A THUG SAVED MY HEART

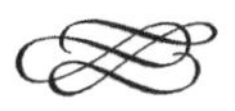

S. YVONNE

Published by S.Yvonne Presents

❀ Created with Vellum

SUBSCRIBE

Interested in keeping up with more releases from S.Yvonne? To be notified first of all upcoming releases, exclusive sneak peaks, and contest to win prizes. Please subscribe to her mailing list by texting Syvonnepresents to 22828

KEEP IN TOUCH

Please feel free to connect with me on social media as well:
Facebook: Author Syvonne Powell
Facebook Like Page: Author S.Yvonne
Facebook VIP Readers Group: Book Tea Bae's
(S.Yvonne's Book Club)
Instagram: Authoress_s.yvonne
Tik Tok: therealsyvonne

LEANDRA 'LELE' WELLS

"Malik! Come on baby we gone be late! I can't be late to my own party! Need I remind you it's gonna be hella traffic tonight cause everybody leaving the game!"

I stood in front of the mirror putting the last touches on my face, which was pretty much my eyeliner and mascara cause that's all I really needed to make my chestnut brown eyes pop. I pulled the satin cap from my head and removed the pink silk wrap so I could comb my long hair down. I had gone to the salon earlier and got a bomb ass Dominican blowout and since my natural unprocessed hair is already long and thick down my back… my shit was laid.

I slid into a simple sheer, tight fitted body suit that hugged my curves and gave my ass the perfect look. Underneath I wore a dark bodysuit that showed a little cleavage and left my ass cheeks out just a little. The way the small crystals splattered all over my suit when the light hit it was sexy as hell and after checking myself for a third time and was satisfied; I put my soft pink lip gloss on my caramel colored lips and turned the bathroom light off. "Malikkk!" I yelled again looking for his ass.

I hated Miami Traffic at nighttime, especially when there was a game at the Hardrock Stadium like tonight. Traffic would be bullshit going down 27th avenue. The only way I could even see the shit working was if we took 441 straight down to 183rd street to get to Studio 183 where my party was at. Turning twenty-two felt just like twenty-one; ain't shit change but the age and every year since I turned 18… Malik always did something for me even when I told him not to.

Our apartment wasn't that big so I knew it wouldn't be hard to find him. Knowing him his ass probably was out on the balcony smoking a blunt when he should've been getting ready. Malik had been the same for years and had been my savior in literally everything. Although he was only two years older than me the man was wise beyond his years, and might I add… fineeee as hell. I remember the first time we ever met. He was in the parking lot of my high school kicking shit with his little brother Majestic; who was a senior like me at the time.

I'd never forget that day. My girls and me lived for the fast life and the dope boys. Malik sat on top of the hood of his black Camaro with the black 24-inch rims decorating the tires. The sun beamed down on his dark brown skin showing every tattoo he had on both of his arms. He wore a white wife beater tee, some black and red Jordan basketball shorts, and the matching J's on his feet. His low-cut Caesar with the deep waves had every other young nigga in the parking lot seasick. The Cuban link around his neck with the Jesus piece medallion was sexy as hell too.

Needless to say we were all sweating the nigga and Majestic knew it too cause although we were watching Malik,

Majestic was watching us looking at us like we were mad thirsty and shit with his stuck-up ass. He thought every young bitch in the school had to chase him cause his big brother was a dope boy and he was spoiled as shit because of that. Not me though, I wasn't chasing his ass. I hated a stuck-up ass nigga. At the time, I didn't have a car. I rode with my friend Abbey to school and she drove a little two door Honda we always parked way in the back of the parking lot so that's where we were going as I clutched the books against my chest.

"Heyyyy Malik..." All my girls cooed walking passed them. All except for me cause my ass wasn't trying to be noticed. Not because he wasn't cute, but because I was the only one that didn't have my hair done and my appointment wasn't until later in the week. I could've kicked my own ass for slipping like that. I had my long hair pulled up in a sloppy bun with some big hoop earrings.

"Wus good..." He nod his head in our direction while speaking to someone on his phone barely paying us any attention, which caused Majestic to laugh at my girls and shake his head.

"I can't stand that damn boy..." I hissed tossing my books in the back of Abbey's car before we parted ways with Kim and Karter... the twins.

Abbey laughed at me and sucked her teeth. "Nobody ain't thinking bout teeny pop ass Majestic, that's why his ass is mad. Talking about he ran through all the girls... no nigga they ran between yo ass and dropped you like a prostitute on 79th street." She was unbothered as hell as she turned the AC on full blast. It was so damn hot outside our clothes were starting to stick to us.

As soon as we pulled off, before we could even make it to the exit gate, Majestic was flagging us down raising curiosity out of us both wondering what he could've wanted. I rolled down my window first. "What?" I frowned as he focused on me instead of Abbey. He acted like he couldn't stand her either.

"Yo watch yo fucking mouth." He looked unbothered like it was nothing. "My brother wants your number." He tossed me his phone so I could put the number in.

Abbey chuckled. "Oh no he didn't just toss that phone in yo lap like he's entitled."

I looked at his phone like it was a piece of shit before picking it up. I tossed it right back not giving a damn whether he caught it or not. "Well I'm sure yo brother got a mouth and you probably lying any damn way." I refused to believe out of all the girls that nigga had just seen he was interested in my young ass on my most raggedy day.

"Now why would I do that?"

"Cause you thirsty as hell too." I rolled the window up and Abbey sped off leaving him standing there while we laughed and talk shit. We didn't head right home afterward cause I hated going straight home. I loved being around my mama, but I hated my fucking stepfather with a passion so we usually just wasted time until he went to his evening job. Besides, Abbey wanted to ride out to Central High to slide up on her new lil boo anyway and then we went to Popeye's to get some chicken and biscuits before heading home.

When I finally did make it home. I hadn't even made it in the house good before there was a knock on the door. I was surprised as hell to see Malik standing in front of me like I owed him something. "What the fuck? Are you crazy?" I gently push him back giving me room to step out on the porch cause I didn't want my mama or brothers in my business. I especially didn't want my stepfather in my business since he hadn't left yet. "What are you doing at my house?" I asked with a bunch of different emotions hoping nobody saw him or noticed that I'd went back out the house.

Malik stood in front of me with confidence. Like he didn't have a care in the world. The way his eyes looked down on me made me nervous as hell, yet he was captivating at the same time. The smell of his YSL tickled my nose. I could even smell the minty gum on his breath. "The fact that I even had to come over here is crazy.... But that's what happens when you send a boy to do a man's job." He chuckled referring to how I played his brother earlier. I peep Majestic sitting in the passenger seat of Malik's car grilling me. I couldn't wait to get to school the next day cause I was going to cuss his ass out for bringing him here.

I rolled my eyes. "Whatever... so what's up?" I asked nervously looking around. "Cause you got to go... you can't be here."

"Cool... cause I got places I need to be anyway." He shrugged. "I need a number to reach you ma." The way his deep voice spoke with so much authority turned my young ass on. Everything in me wanted to hop up and just kiss all over his baby face since he didn't have any facial hairs.

"For what?" I frowned. "I know you got plenty hoes so what the fuck you want with my young ass?"

"First of all watch yo mouth ma, that shit aint lady like... and for two, I need the number so I can let you know when to be ready for our date. Damn, women always asking questions knowing you gonna give me the number anyway." He shook his head with a smirk on his face.

"LELE!!!!" I heard my mama yell from the door behind me looking for me.

"Un Un... you gotta go before you get me in trouble." I tried pushing him off the porch.

He barely budged. "Number first."

With panic in my voice, I called off the number. "3052613667... now bye!"

I hurriedly walked in the house closing the door behind me and locking it. As soon as I turned around my mama was standing there looking at me like I was crazy. "What were you doing?" She had her eyes squint like she knew I was up to some shit.

"Nothing..." I mumbled. "Throwing something in the garbage outside." I lied while walking around her.

"Um hmmm..." she replied. "Well I'm going to the casino so go cook for George for me." She spoke of my stepfather. "I took out some chicken, it's in the sink."

With that she grabbed her keys and left. I rolled my eyes so fucking hard in the back of my head. I was expecting his nagging ass to go to work but now here I was about to have to serve him dinner and hear his mouth the rest of the night about boys and homework. The dishes were all over the sink since they never made my brothers Leon and Latrell do shit and before I could start cooking, I had to wash them. I must've broken at least three dishes in the process the way I was slamming shit.

"WHAT THE FUCK LELE!" I heard George yell from the back room scuffling around getting ready to come check my ass. At the same time, a text came through on my phone from Malik asking if I could get out of the house. I was surprised that he even remembered the number. I heard George's footsteps coming down the hall. Since I was probably gonna get grounded for breaking up the damn dishes anyway, I said fuck it.

I hurriedly sent Malik a text back telling him to meet me on the corner. I grabbed my house keys and my coat from by the front door and ran up outta there. "LELEEE!" I heard George coming for me. I didn't give a shit... I was outta there running all the way to the corner where Malik was already waiting for me.

"Go! Hurry up!" I rushed him looking back to make sure it was clear.

He hit the gas driving with one hand while looking at me shaking my head. He chuckled. "What you do?"

Settling in his butter leather passenger seat. I shrugged. "Nothing the average teenager hasn't done." When I looked at him, he was staring at me like he was reading me or something. "Whatttt?"

He chuckled before turning up the music. "Nothing... I see Imma have to watch yo ass."

I didn't know what that had meant, but it was pointless trying to address it because the music was so damn loud. After that though, we were always together and it took some time for my parents to get used to it since they were against me having a boyfriend until after I graduated. No matter how much they bitched, they couldn't help but to take a liking to Malik.

If I needed my hair done, he took me. Needed clothes, he bought them. Needed money in my pocket, he provided. Always made sure I was home by curfew, and was always looking out for my little brothers. Although they were only Freshman they looked up to Malik. Deep down inside, I knew my peoples knew Malik was a dope boy but they never addressed it. My young ass had been hit by the love bug and didn't care what nobody felt about it.

In the beginning, he wasn't shit though. He treated me good but he had plenty hoes hating my young ass cause they just couldn't see what he wanted with me that they didn't have. I'd caught him cheating so many times it wasn't even funny. I even lost count of all the fights I had with bitches. It eventually died down though and I held it down cause I loved my man.

I found Malik out on the balcony just like I knew I would. As soon as I opened the sliding door, the cool night breeze kissed my face. His favorite YSL cologne tickled my nose mixed with weed. That shit smelled so good. As soon as he heard me, he turned around and motioned for me to come sit on his lap while he smoked and finished his conversation. "No nigga… I'm telling you now. My shit better be right or niggas gone have to see me. Nigga's gettin' too comfortable round this muthafucka. Them lil niggas on 135th just beggin' to be caught much as attention they draw to themselves." He sighed shaking his head. He pulled on the blunt again before passing it to me.

I put it to my lips and took a soft pull before closing my eyes and exhaling. Malik was watching me intensely as he used one of his fingers circling it on my hard nipple through my thin fabric causing me to blush. I leaned over kissing his lips feeling his dick coming alive under me. My man looked the fuck good rocking a full Gucci outfit with the matching shoes. He'd let his beard grow in and it was lined up perfectly. His toned muscles turned me the fuck on. On the left side of his neck, he had my name in cursive letters 'Leandra'.

On my left wrist I had his name. I also had his name on my lower back right above my ass too. Abbey thought I was stupid for getting a niggas name on me but I didn't give a fuck cause the world was gone know. "We have to go…" I whispered in his ear before brushing my tongue across his lope.

He nodded his head as he finished his conversation while cupping my ass. The more I fucked with him the harder his dick became and the more my pussy throbbed. Had my body suit been easy access I would've surely fucked him right here on the balcony, but because it wasn't… I decided to treat my man. Squatting down in between his legs, I used my freshly manicured hand to pull his thick mane from out of his jeans. One look at it and my mouth was watering. I could literally feel the throbbing in my hands from his thick vein.

We locked eyes one more time before he gave me a knowing look. With one motion, I made sure my mouth was extra wet before slowly taking the tip of his dick in my mouth where I focused on the head. I felt Malik tense up a little bit trying to hold his composure as he tried to continue to listen to what the person on the phone was telling him. I gripped his dick and started deep throating that shit while massaging his balls at the same time making sure to sip, slurp, and gag while I was at it every time I put it to the back of my throat. With my free hand, I massaged his balls not giving a shit who may have been watching. Malik put his phone on mute with his eyes closed. "Ssssss… damn baby." He pumped furiously in my mouth until his semen was exploding inside my mouth.

I literally tried to suck the soul out of him. I swallowed all of his babies and then innocently looked into his eyes. "Come here…" he pulled me up to him kissing me deeply on my lips. I kissed him hard before winking at him signaling I'd be back. Whoever he had been talking to had long hung up.

"Come let me clean you up." I grabbed him by the hand. When we made it in the bathroom Malik just stared at me as I cleaned him off.

"What?" I giggled. "You know that shit makes me nervous."

He looked me dead in the eyes. "I want some pussy LeLe… you can't give a nigga that kinda dome and think he ain't gone want no pussy behind it ma." Malik was trying to get my damn bodysuit off and I wasn't having it.

"Un Un… hellll no! We already late, which was my reason for coming out there to get you anyway. I promise I got you later baby, but we have to go!" I zipped his pants and rushed out the bathroom. Malik wasn't too happy with me but I knew he would get over it. He had spent way too much money at that damn club for us to miss it. By the time we made it out of the apartment it was almost midnight and my phone was blowing up. Abbey, Kim, and Karter… all my bitches were calling me.

Instead of picking up, I silenced the calls cause I didn't feel like getting cussed out and this shit wasn't even all my fault. "Where we going?" I questioned Malik when I realized we were in my parents' neighborhood.

He focused on the road like he had a lot on his mind. "I gotta make one run ma, chill with all the questions."

"Malikkkkk….." I whined. "Oh my God man we are so late… this is so embarrassing." I squealed sinking down into the seat getting pissed off. "Just take me home."

"What?!" He snapped looking at me with his brows furrowed.

I fold my arms across my chest pouting. "Just take me home. I'm not going. This is so embarrassing. I'm sure they done drunk up all the liquor and ate all the food."

"Niggas know don't shit shake till I get there… got me fucked up. I'm not taking you home so you might as well just fix ya lil attitude." He replied nonchalantly like he always did. I was getting ready to say something else until we pulled up in my mama's yard and a whole bunch of cars were parked outside.

"What's this?" I frowned.

He shut the engine off of his Audi A7 and hopped out coming around to my side to open the door and let me out.

We didn't have time for this but I wasn't even about to keep talking shit cause he was gone do what he wanted anyway.

"Quick ma… this gone be real quick… this the first part of your birthday gift." He assured me before walking me inside.

LEANDRA 'LELE' WELLS

As soon as he walked me in the lights came on and confetti was being popped all over the front living room. "SURPRISEEE!" Everyone yelled catching me off guard. My mama, George, Leon, Latrell, Abbey, Kim, Karter, and a lot more of family and friends. Mrs. Jones, Malik's mama was here too… so was Majestic.

There was a cake in the middle of the dining room table and everyone was holding a single white rose in their hands. My mama had tears in her eyes and I didn't know why she was so damn emotional. I hugged everybody and wanted to thank Malik but as soon as I turned around to do that. I look down and he was on one knee staring up at me as the music started playing Wale's song Matrimony.

If there's a question of my heart, you've got it. It don't belong to anyone but you. If there's a question of my love, you've got it. Baby don't worry, I got plans for you. Baby I've been making plans, oh love. Baby, I've been making plans for you. Baby, I've been making plans. Baby, I've been making plans for you.

The love of my life was looking at me with so much love

in his eyes it scared me. The way our energy gravitated toward each other was crazy. Instantly the tears started cascading down my face and everyone who knew me knew that I wasn't an emotional ass female. This was just on a whole other level. "LeLe… from the first day I laid eyes on you in the parking lot of your school, I knew you was gone be the one for me. You were with other females all dressed up, hair done, nails done and everything else but on that day you rocked a sloppy bun and basic clothes just simple and natural beauty surrounded you. I've loved you since day one ma, and the shit ain't ever going anywhere. I dedicate my life to making sure you happy and we good. You make me happy. You care for me unselfishly. You know what I need without me having to ask and I adore you for that. So today, in front of all the people who matter the most. I wanna ask you to be my future wife. Leandra Wells… will you marry me?"

I don't even think he got the words out good before I was down with him wrapping my arms around his neck hugging him. The emotions that overcame me wouldn't even let me speak cause I was too busy crying like a baby while trying to hide my face in his neck. "Well damn is that a yes or no?" Karter asked from behind me as everyone cheered and laughed. That was just like Karter's loudmouth ass. I didn't know who was worse out of her and Kim.

"Yes, yes, yes. I'll marry you!" I beamed kissing his lips.

Malik slid the iced-out rock on my finger as soon as I gave him the okay. "Bout time, nigga knees all cramped up waiting on an answer. Almost thought you were bout to say no. I was goin' straight home to change the locks." He joked admiring the ring causing everyone else to laugh in an uproar.

"I'm so happy for ya'll… my babies." My mama cooed all over us. Today she was wearing her blonde short cut wig, her long exotic lashes, and the bright red lipstick on her lips.

Couldn't tell her shit. I was so glad my mama was still young and hip cause we talked about everything and she understood me.

Malik slipped off on the other side of the living room in a huddle of man talk with Leon, Latrell, and Majestic. I briefly wondered what that was about but I didn't have time to be nosy. My twin brothers had changed drastically over the years. At eighteen years old they both were cute as hell with that perfect Miami swag. Leon wore his hair cut low while Latrell had the long neat dread Locs. They both were 6'2 in height with dark chocolate skin, but had a totally different taste in what they wanted out of life. Leon was the star basketball player at Central High and Latrell was the star quarterback on the football field. One thing they did have in common was them both wanting to play college ball.

I was headed over to speak with my crew when George stopped me. I smelled his aftershave before he even spoke. Although we'd had a rough few years; at some point I realized that he only wanted what was best for me and I gave his ass hell. "I want you to know that you turned out to be a fine young lady and I'm so proud of you." He told me with his eyes watered up. "I know you never looked at me like your real father; but I always looked at you like my biological daughter and I'm very happy for you Leandra." He hugged me.

Now I wasn't expecting to tear up but I did. Dammit, had me crying again. "Thank you so much for everything George. I know I gave you hell but thank you for stepping in and caring for kids you didn't make."

"Wouldn't have it any other way." He replied removing his glasses using his fingers to wipe the corners of his wet eyes. "Next stop graduation right?"

I knew he wanted to see where my head was at but this

wasn't going to change anything. I had worked too hard at Miami Dade College to get my degree in business management and I wasn't giving it up for no nigga. My time was so close I could smell it. "Of course." I assured him.

He nodded his head placing one hand on my shoulder. "Good girl."

Kim, Karter, and Abbey surrounded me boasting over my ring. "Bitchhh look at that shit." Abbey whispered in my ear low enough for my mama them to not hear her.

"I knowww it's so bomb." Karter and Kim chimed in unison. These bitches were the prettiest twins I'd ever seen in my life. They looked like chocolate Barbies with long beautiful hair. Nice bodies and beautiful smiles. They were 5'4 in height which is an inch under me since I'm 5'5 and they were wild as fuck. Abbey stood right next to them and taller than us all. Her light skin and freckles is what stood out the most about her, right along with that sandy brown hair of hers. Although we love to party, we all made sure we attended school cause one thing we weren't ever trying to do was be dependent on a nigga to fend for us.

"Yes it is but I've got a party to get to! Ya'll ready or what? Cause I'm ready to get fucked up." I told them looking for Malik. Abbey and Karter followed me but not Kim. "What's the deal with her?" I frowned.

Karter shrugged. "You know how she is… just weird as fuck. It's like she'll be happy for you but at the same time feel jealous cause it ain't her."

"Um hmm." Abbey agreed. "You know she been like that since middle school. She wants to be the first one to experience everything. She'll be aiight tho."

I wasn't dare wasting time to respond. I loved Kim but she's one of those friends you had to watch harder than an enemy sometime. "Bae it's time to go." I told Malik interrupting his conversation.

"Can't believe you bout to force a nigga to call her my sister." Majestic's hating ass told Malik.

"Nigga shut up." I chuckled. We had gotten way better over the years. He wasn't the same stuck up ass nigga from high school. He'd changed a lot but was still talking shit to everybody.

Malik pulled me close to him cupping a handful of my ass in his hands. He made sure that he had his back toward everybody so they couldn't see what he was doing. Nuzzling his nose in the side of my neck he gently sucked there and then let go. "Come on, we bout to head out now baby… you gotta say goodnight to everybody."

I did exactly what he said in within the next twenty minutes we were headed out and walking in the club. All the old heads stayed at my mama's house but all the young people including my brothers were hanging with us tonight at the party. When I walked in the building was lit. Malik had rented out a small personal section for us where the bottles were coming all night long. I was surprised to see Malik was actually fucked up cause he never drank like that when we were out, but tonight… I guess he was truly celebrating making me his future wife.

When it was time to leave the club, I demanded him to give me the keys and I drive home cause although we were both fucked up… I felt I was more sober than he was. He knew he was fucked up so he didn't even put up much of a fight. "On the real ma… I think somebody put some shit in those drinks or they replaced the good shit with some cheap shit." He slurred down in the passenger seat putting the air directly in his face before closing his eyes.

I put the seatbelt on and slowly pulled off. Looking over

at Malik; I smiled at his sexy face and grabbed his hand into mine as I used my left hand to drive. I couldn't wait to get home though cause I felt like I was okay until I sat down and the liquor really start setting in. Fighting to keep my eyes open; I turned the music up loud anticipating seeing my street soon. I was regretting driving now. We should've taken a damn Uber or rode with somebody else and the way Malik was over there snoring had me jealous as fuck.

I'm not sure what happened, maybe I dozed off briefly but when I opened my eyes, I was swerving and tried to avoid hitting another car head on since I was on the wrong side of the road. "Oh my God! Malik!" I squealed right before hitting a pole causing the entire car to flip. I felt and excruciating pain in my shoulder and an instant pain in my head. The airbags deployed causing a loud noise and I prayed. Prayed for God to wrap his arms around us both. I wanted it to be over. The only thing I could hear were the sounds of horns blowing, tires screeching, and twisted metal before everything went black.

LEANDRA 'LELE' WELLS

Beep. Beep. Beep. Beep.

I woke up in a daze to the sound of the I.V machine right next to me on the side of my hospital bed. My head was in excruciating pain and my left shoulder was in a sling. Looking around, it took a minute for my vision to focus but when I did; my mama was sitting there staring at me with tears in her eyes. She slowly made her way to the bed when she saw me awake staring at her. "Oh my God LeLe… thank God you're okay." She cried standing over me. She looked like she'd been crying for days with puffy eyes.

I tried to sit up but winced in pain from my shoulder. I remembered there was an accident but that's it. What led up to it… I truly didn't know. "What happen mama?" I asked barely above a whisper since my throat was so dry. I felt the taste of blood in my mouth. That's when I realized the inside of my lip was busted and swollen. So was my left eye. I didn't even want to address the lump I felt on top of my forehead.

She stared at me with sympathy in her eyes. "LeLe… you

ran off the road baby. Your blood alcohol level was extremely over the limit and you shouldn't have been driving."

The tears instantly ran down my face. "Ma... where's Malik? How can I be so stupid." I cried. "I know he's so mad at me right now."

"I... I... I..." She adverted her eyes away from mine fidgeting with her fingers refusing to look at me.

"Ma! What??? He can't hate me that bad! I need to see him! Is he okay?" I panic just feeling like I needed to explain myself for being so irresponsible.

"Um LeLe... Malik... he didn't make it baby." She burst into hard tears.

My mind went blank at first. There wasn't a reaction cause I knew what she said was bullshit. As she cried; I laughed loud and hard. A good laugh too before I questioned her again. She was looking at me like I'd lost my mind. "No forreal mama." I finally stopped laughing. "Where is he?" The look she gave me scared me almost to my death. That's when I knew... I knew what she was telling me was real as my chest caved in.

"The car flipped and he was ejected from the vehicle. When he landed and broke a rib it pierced his heart killing him on the scene. He was pronounced dead when the paramedics arrived baby. There was nothing they could do."

I heard what she was telling me and although she was standing right next to me. It was like her words were traveling from a distance and I couldn't wrap my mind around what she was saying. I didn't even realize I was screaming until the staff ran in to calm me down. "NOOOO! NOOOO! NOOOO!" I cried ignoring all of my own pain. I literally felt like somebody had ripped my entire heart from my chest. "THAT'S A LIE!!!" I bawled out. "Tell me you lying! GO

GET HIM RIGHT NOW! TELL HIM TO WAKE UP! HE GOTTA WAKE UP!"

"Ms. Wells we need you to try to calm down." One of the nurses told me. "We understand you're upset but you're very fragile right now."

"LeLe please…" my mama begged.

I didn't want to hear none of the shit they were saying. Fuck my condition. "Ya'll better go get him right the fuck now!"

The entire room was in an uproar as they held me down injecting something in my vein. I felt myself floating with visions of Malik's face in my mind before I drifted off. When I came to, the room was quiet but my heart was hurting so bad. I was alone this time so I pressed the button on the remote for a nurse or doctor to come in.

An older black man with a head full of grey hairs walked in. He looked at me with his deep brown eyes as he read my chart before standing next to me. "Ms. Wells… I'm doctor Joseph. I'll be looking after you for the night. How are you feeling?" He asked a dumb ass question.

I blankly stared at the ceiling not saying anything at all. I had nothing to say and too depressed and hurt to talk. My brain was still trying to wrap everything around it.

"I understand…" He looked at me sympathetic. "You don't have to speak right now. I'm sure this must be very hard for you. I just want to make sure we keep you relaxed that's why we've got you on a high dosage of pain meds through your I.V."

"What happened to me?" I managed to ask.

"Outside of a busted lip and a few bruises, you did suffer a mild concussion, and a broken shoulder blade. However, we couldn't save the fetus. We tried but with you being so early on we couldn't save it."

My eyes shot to him as my breathing slowed down and I tried to catch my breath. "Fetus?" I asked with trembling lips. "What fetus?"

Doctor Joseph looked over the report again. "I apologize… I wasn't aware you didn't know, but upon arrival it was discovered you were almost 3 months pregnant."

More tears as I closed my eyes. I had always had an irregular period. Never in a million years did I think I was pregnant. I felt fine prior to this. To know that I lost the love of my life and my baby all in one was too much for me. I knew I'd never be the same after this. I held my hand up to stop him from talking to me. "Please…" I whispered. "Please… I need a minute."

He simply nodded his head looking as if he felt sorry for me and walked out assuring me that he would give me a few minutes and come back. My soul hurt so bad for the pain I'd caused myself and everybody else who knew what was going on. I especially cried for Malik cause because of me he lost his life. How dare me put a seatbelt on myself and not make sure he had his on as well. I'm sure that's the only thing that saved me. I cried so badly it hurt. I'd do anything to get him back… anything! For the rest of the night, I cried and refused to talk to anybody. Even when my mama and Abbey came to sit with me… I just couldn't.

LEANDRA 'LELE' WELLS

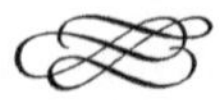

It had been a month since the accident and I couldn't even go to Malik's funeral. Everyone around me tried to keep me in good spirits telling me it wasn't my fault; it was just an accident but I couldn't forgive myself. My days were dark as hell as I mourned the loss of my man and our unborn child. I had fallen into a deep depression. I hadn't been to class. I didn't take any calls and most of the time I slept. Since I couldn't bear staying in our apartment; I broke the lease and moved back into my mama's house.

Leon and Latrell kept me company when they weren't running the streets and my mama and George did everything else for me… especially since I was still recovering from my shoulder injury. Today I sat in the living room with a pair of black tights on, black slouch socks, a black hoodie, and blanket wrapped around my body. I was alone and glad that I had the time to just think. I missed Malik so much it hurt. I couldn't even bear going to his funeral because I knew my heart couldn't take it. I stared down at my engagement ring that I was still wearing and wiped a lone tear that fell down my left cheek.

Knock. Knock. Knock.

I almost ignored the door but then I remembered my mama telling me she had been waiting on a package from Amazon. When I opened the door, much to my surprise it was two uniformed officers staring me in the face. "Can I help you?" I asked.

"Leandra Nicole Wells…" the shorter one of the two male officers said.

"Yes… that's me… can I help you?"

"Can you step outside with us ma'am" He asked.

I did as I was told thinking they wanted to question me about some shit that probably happened in the neighborhood. "Is everything okay?"

He pulled out his cuffs while the other one flashed the warrant. "Leandra Wells you're under arrest for DUI/Manslaughter resulting in the death of Mr. Malik Jones. You have the right to remain silent. Anything you say can be used against you in the court of law. You have the right to talk to a lawyer for advice before we ask you any questions. You have the right to have a lawyer with you during the questioning. If you do not have a lawyer one will be appointed to you…." He continued on but at this point I had blanked the fuck out.

I couldn't believe this shit. As if I hadn't suffered enough, I was being charged with Malik's death. I never in a million years imagined the state filing charges against me. Because my shoulder was still fucked up and couldn't wrap around my back, they cuffed me from the front, shackled my ankles and hauled me off in the unmarked police vehicle while everyone on our block watched.

Two hours later, I was processed and waiting to use the

phone in a funky ass brown uniform. Jail wasn't a place for me, these bitches looked rough. Crack heads, scammers, and straight up shooters. My eyes scanned the small holding cell and landed on a group of females in prayer group. The tallest of the women, a skinny blonde head and a missing front tooth caught me staring and ask if I wanted to join. Shaking my head, I scrambled off to the other side and sat down with my knees tucked and pulled up to my chest. A deputy came in with one trustee pushing a tray of cold dry looking sandwiches to pass out. I didn't wanna eat shit, but I didn't decline just in case I may have needed it later.

Seems like it took forever but my mama came through for me. My bond was $100,000 because of my charges in which $10,000 of that had to be paid with a bondsmen. I didn't know where the hell she got that money from but I didn't dare ask. I'm just glad I didn't have to sit in jail for more than a week cause those three days alone killed me. The worst three days of my life outside of losing Malik. I didn't do shit besides cry. Literally all day. On top of trying to deal with a broken heart. I had to deal with this case now. Ironically though, I'd made peace with whatever they decided to do with me. Most times, I sat in the dark convincing myself that I should pay for what I had done to him.

"LeLe!" Latrell plopped down next to me on the couch snapping me out of my thoughts.

"Huh?" I blinked. "What? What happen?"

Latrell was looking at me like I was crazy sitting next to me wearing an Armani outfit. Something had looked different about him. Something was different about his swag. His demeanor. The way he was carrying himself. I just couldn't put a finger on it. He smelled like weed too… and YSL. Shit brought tears to my eyes remembering that's exactly how Malik used to smell. I wanted to gag knowing I couldn't see him anymore, and anything that reminded me of him made me sick. "You gone drive yourself crazy sis… I know you still grieving but you gotta get out this house." He pulled some wrap from his pocket and started breaking down the weed right in front of me.

"Since when you started doing that?" I asked with an eyebrow raised. Although our parents weren't home. It's the principal of the matter.

He chuckled and shook his head while ignoring my question. "Look, I just want you to keep your head up shawty. You my big sis and I'm just not used to seeing you so down like this. Like, you aint even yoself."

I nibbled on my bottle lip thinking about what he was saying, but he didn't know what this shit was like. "Yeah, I hear you… but you aint in this situation Trell." I told him just as my phone rang. It was Kim, I ignored it.

His eyes scan down to the phone. "You aint even been hollerin' at ya partna them…"

He was agitating the shit out of me right now. "I have bigger problems aiight." I sucked my teeth and stood up to walk in the back room.

"I get that but…"

"But nothing! Nobody knows what this shit feels like but everybody wanna tell me what the fuck to do! I gotta go see what this lawyer talking about tomorrow! I could be going to jail and you wanna talk to me bout some bitches!" I referred to my friends. I didn't even mean what the fuck I was saying. I was just hurting. I slammed the door to my room and looked out the window. Shortly after, I heard the front door open and close.

Majestic was parked in the front yard. Through his front windshield, I could see him looking at me as we locked eyes. The way he was looking at me scared me to death. I didn't even know how to make out. I swallowed hard and exhaled.

With the blink of an eye, his frown turned into a smile and he gave me a slight wave like he normally would. I waved back. He couldn't fool me though. Even through that smile. I could see the hurt. For this, I didn't trust Majestic. Now, I wasn't so sure that I trust my brother around him either. Even Mrs. Jones was acting kind of funny with me. I didn't mean to hurt anybody, I just hoped they could forgive me one day and be real about it cause the way I was feeling. They were all showing me two faces.

* * *

I SAT in the hired attorney's office chewing on my bottom lip while she went through some papers. The anxiety of waiting to see what she was gonna say was killing me. On one side of me was my mama holding my hand. George sat on the other side of me looking straight ahead. I was just glad they didn't let me come alone. Mrs. Ransom, my attorney was a beautiful black woman looked to be in her mid 40's. The crème suit she wore was sharp and her perfectly manicured nails stood out, especially with that rock on her finger. She looked like money and got straight to the point.

"Okay Ms. Wells. I'm going to just be as honest as possible with you. As your attorney, I work for you, so whatever decision you make, I'm here to represent you every step of the way." She nodded her head looking me in the eyes. "Now, the District Attorney has made an offer..." She shuffled through the papers. "As you know, you're being charged with a DUI resulting in manslaughter." She waited for my response to make sure I was fully aware.

"Yes..." I nodded my head in agreement letting her know I understood. "If I plead not guilty then what happens?"

"You take it to trial..." She responded. "However, if you

take it to trial and we don't win; they are ready to hit you with the minimum of 20 years."

My heart dropped. I felt my mama squeeze my hand even tighter. George still sat with a stern face but I could just feel the hurt bouncing from his body. "And what's the offer if I do plead guilty?"

"Five years state prison, due to the guidelines… you'll do 2 ½ years at the least."

I didn't wait for anyone to consult what my answer should be cause that was a no brainer. I felt the warm tears surround my eyes before a single tear fell. "I'll take the plea."

Everything after that just went fast. I'll never forget the way my mama screeched out loud as she cried, or the way George grabbed his chest with just the mere thought of me having to go to prison. I cried and cried my damn self. However, it was the best thing to do and I had to pay for what I'd done.

My heart broke in a million more pieces but I loved that man just enough to suck my own feelings up. I did the crime so I had to do the time. I just prayed I could forgive myself like I knew he did.

5 1/2 YEARS LATER

Chapter 5 (2 ½ Years Later)

MAJESTIC JONES

"I know muthafuckin well you ain't let no lil niggas slide in my place of business and just rob shit!" Poochie paced back and forth in front of me in his isolated warehouse. Shit was huge, but I was smart enough to know that a big shot caller like him was holding no weight here cause if he was; I wouldn't be standing in this muthafucka. It was my own fault though for even being in the nigga presence cause I fucked up. Poochie was what the bitches would call 'an old pretty ass nigga' but he was deadly outside of all that. The city of Miami knew, if bricks were moving... Poochie's name was somewhere in it. Only few knew him by his street name and he kept it that way.

Although he had multiple businesses outside of this shit. I just felt like it was his obsession with needing power that kept him in the game. Everybody did as much as possible to avoid him, but my stupid ass got caught slipping and now here I was. My eyes scanned the warehouse. To the naked eye, one would think he was alone but I knew better. He had at least 3 or 4 snipers in this bitch. "Poochie, I had no idea that shit was going down man, you gotta believe me. You think if I knew them young niggas was stealing out the spot I would've even walked away for a second?" I tried to reason.

He stopped and looked at me with death in his eyes. "Nigga, why the fuck you walk away in the first place? What the fuck do I pay you for nigga?" I watched him open up a toolbox with a bunch of screwdrivers and shit in it.

"I'mma handle it bro, I promise you that." I assured him. I didn't need shit getting out of hand. It had even been an honor to be working for the nigga, and he only gave me a job off the strength of Malik after he died.

"Oh, I know you gone handle it!" He shook his head and blew out a whistle that echoed throughout the warehouse. Within a few minutes two of the big niggas that worked for him were bringing out two of my lil niggas I had working under me. The two that got caught stealing. Raymond and Quez. Niggas had me out here looking stupid for trusting they lil bitch asses. "Sit these lil niggas down." He ordered. I watched Poochie take off the wool pleaded bags they both had covering their heads. When they saw us they both looked like they wanted to shit on themselves. Poochie pulled up a chair and sat directly in front of them. "I ain't gotta ask questions. Ya'll know why ya'll here."

Raymond went to rambling first pleading for his life. "Look big dawg I'm sorry man. Please don't kill me! I ain't think it was a big deal. I swear I was gone put the shit back in a few days." He looked like a whole bitch with tears cascading down his face. "Why the nigga Mondo ain't in here? He took some too!" He started calling names like a muthafucka. This was a bad sign. A real bad sign.

Quez frowned with his nostrils flared. "Nigga shut the fuck up!" He tried to warn his homie and do damage control. He sucked up all his fear and spoke directly to Poochie looking at him in the eyes like a man. "You gone kill me anyway so fuck it. I took the money cause my grandma is sick and don't nobody take care of her but me. They cut her social security check short and I needed the extra bread, but I swear I was gone put the shit back in a few days. I mean, if this nigga was paying us proper instead of penny pitching anyway then this shit wouldn't have even happened."

Poochie calmly nodded his head but I was heated. "What the fuck? Nigga is you crazy?" I slapped his ass like the bitch he was acting like. "Lil Nigga I pay you for what the fuck you do… the bare fucking minimum."

Poochie gave me a glare. "Control yoself in my establishment. Nigga you aint callin' no shots in here." He warned me. He stood up out of his chair and walked around them both. "I hear you lil nigga. I can respect an honest man. What I don't respect is a thief… that's the worst kinda man. A real man ain't gone steal from another. He gone handle up and go out there and get it. If you had a problem you should've hollered at me directly before you made those kinda decisions. For that mistake you gotta pay."

He pulled out his burner from the small of his back. Pow! He put a single bullet through Raymond's scull causing blood to splatter all over us all. Quez jumped and closed his eyes preparing for it to be him next. "You know why he had to die?" Poochie asked Quez and then answered his own question. "Look how quick it was for that nigga to start name calling. He's a fucking rat. If he can sit here in my face and rat out other niggas to save his own life; imagine what the fuck he will tell the laws?"

Quez was shaking but nod his head in agreement. "Watch the niggas you have around you." He told him. "Where's the bread?" He asked him.

"I.. I.. still gotta get it up. But I swear I'll have it in a few days."

"You sure will… you gotta give that back. It wasn't yours to take." Poochie told him. "Only reason I'mma let you live is cause you got heart. You ain't fold like yo weak ass homeboy over here." He referred to Raymond as he slouched over life-less. I wanted to fucking gag the way that shit turned my stomach. Malik would've never handled business like this but to each its own. Before Quez could even speak his gratitude, Poochie aimed his gun at his hand and shot him there instead.

"AHHHH!" He yelled out in pain.

"Don't ever take shit from me again." He growled. "Now get the fuck outta here before I change my mind." One of the big niggas led Quez out as he cried holding his hand. He then looked at me. "Who is his family?" Referring to Raymond.

"His mama and lil sister." I told him.

He handed me a bag with a few stacks in it. "When they find his body… make sure you give them this bread so they can bury him." He ordered and then told the other nigga. "Clean this shit up."

I took the bag and walked off.

"Yo!" He called behind me. "Keep ya soldiers in order or next time it's gone be you my nigga."

I understood, cause it was definitely my fuck up that's why I aint say shit. I walked outside to the hot ass sun greeting me. Popping the trunk, I tossed the bag of money and then hopped in my whip before peeling off. I knew what the fuck my problem was. I needed a new line up and I knew exactly who. I picked up my cell and called Latrell. "Yo, what's good my G?"

"Shit can't call it… still balling on the field and fucking these college hoes." He laughed. Him and Leon were in their Junior year at University of Miami.

"Shit ain't nothing wrong with that." I made a turn on 79th

street coming out of the industrial area. "You still tryna make some money?"

"Helll yeah… what the play is?"

"Get with Leon and meet me tonight. Usual Spot…"

"Bet." He hung up.

My mind was all over the place as I pulled up to my mama's house. Still looked the same from when we were growing up besides some minor renovations. Since I solely took care of her now, I had to grind extra hard. Since the death of Malik, she hadn't been the same. Stopped working and all. I swear she loved that nigga more than she loves me. When Malik was alive she would do anything for him… when it comes to me though; shit was like pulling teeth.

"Ma!" I yelled her name using my key to walk inside. I followed the smell of fried pork chops coming from the kitchen. There she was staring at the pan cooking. I kissed her on the cheek. "Hey ma…"

"Hey baby…" She spoke without looking. The bags under her eyes were an indication to me that she hadn't slept much. Shit broke my heart to see her looking so weary. "You hungry?"

"Yeah…" I grabbed the mail off the counter. "Let me get one of those pork chops sandwiches." I scanned my mail. I wanted her to hurry up cause her house made a nigga depressed sometimes. She had her days where she was talking shit and her days where she barely said shit at all.

She fixed the sandwich for me making sure she drowned it in hot sauce like I liked it and then she sat down at the table and started eating her food. "I need some money Majestic."

"Ma, I just paid yo rent and gave you money last week. You don't even leave the house so I know damn well you don't need no money." I stopped chewing briefly just to stare at her. Still the prettiest woman in the world to me. Dark honey skin, pretty kinky hair and all.

"Yeah, well I need it." She snapped standing up walking to grab her bottle of Tequila from the cabinet. She aint even bother to get a cup or nothing. She took the shit straight from the bottle and downed it. Another one of her fucking problems. Shit got on my last fucking nerve. "Malik never asked me questioned bout no money! Don't you fucking start nigga! I carried your ass for 9 months, 2 weeks, 1 day, and 36 hours of motherfucking labor! I should be able to get whatever the fuck I want!" She sassed taking another swig.

I couldn't believe this shit. Couldn't even argue just shook my head. "You can compare me to him all you want and it still aint gone bring him back." Shit still broke my heart till this very day, but I couldn't lash out on my mama because of that. In my eyes, we were all we got. Wish she would see that shit too. Everything I did for her, she made me feel like I was competing with Malik. She was always on one, but today was different.

I didn't even feel like eating my sandwich no more. I sat that shit on the counter and stepped away so I could answer the phone. "Yo…"

"Change of plans my boi…." Latrell said. "We can't meet tonight but I'll keep you posted."

I furrowed my brows and wiped one hand down my face. I didn't have the patience for this shit. "Look, you said you wanted to get paid and I'm tryna help you. Either you want this money or not cause aint shit more important than that paper."

"Nigga, chill the fuck out aiight. Change of plans. LeLe was coming home in the morning. She's getting out late tonight instead and we gotta go get her. If the offer still stands I'll fuck wit'chu tomorrow and if not then better luck next time but don't shit come before me being there for her when the gates open."

I felt a tighten in my chest. This explained why the fuck I was so off my shit today. I knew it was something. I looked back at my mama. Now it made sense why she was acting the worse today. "Aiight my nigga… tell LeLe I'll come check her when she get settled. You holla at me when you done doing the family shit." I told him before hanging up.

I pulled a wad of twenties wrapped in a rubber band from my pocket and sat it on the table. Kissing my mama again, she rolled her eyes. I didn't have shit to say. I just walked out.

ABBEY DANIELS

I had one hand on my hip and the other one I used my pointer finger to mush Latrell right in the middle of the forehead. "Nigga, I can't believe you forgot she was getting out late tonight. You knew this." I fussed his little fine ass out. As soon as I found out a few weeks ago that my bitch was coming home; I started making plans for a welcome home party. I'd rented out Jazzy's Hookah Lounge that specialized in Hookah and soul food. I didn't know who owned the spot but I wanted to personally shake their hand and let them know that they were doing the damn thing. The food was so damn good it made me wanna slap anybody's fucking mama.

"Yo, stop fucking putting yo hands on me Abbey. I be telling ya'll bout that shit." Trell chuckled before shaking his head. "You know damn well I didn't forget." He lied. I could tell he was lying too… but whatever. He was here now and that's all that mattered. "Where Leon?" He asked as he scanned the room for his twin.

I shrugged. "Who knows, probably with some bitch but he better get his ass here. I still need a lot of help." I looked down at my watch. Although her coming home party wasn't until tomorrow. The owners were nice enough to let us decorate tonight so we could just come right in tomorrow afternoon without worrying about all this extra stuff. I rushed from my job and came right over. Being a certified physical therapist had me working long hours at times but my paycheck was worth it. Especially since I liked expensive shit. "Grab those chairs and put them around those tables for me. "I pointed and sent him on his way.

"Kim…" I walked up on her just as she was finishing a balloon arch. She had gotten good over the years. Outside of working as a personal trainer, on the side she did party décor. Actually any occasion that anybody needed she could deliver. "You okay over here?"

She rolled her eyes and sighed. "Girl go head on; I could do this shit with my eyes closed." She tried to wave me off. Kim was looking damn good. Her personal training was really paying off too. In my opinion, she looked she could've been Bernice Burgos little sister or some sort of relative.

I laughed. "Aiight, aiight… you spoke to Karter? Is she coming down?" I asked. Karter had moved to Orlando with her fiancé after college and was expecting a new baby in a few months. None of us knew what the gender was cause she wouldn't tell it though. As a matter of fact she kept a lot of her personal life private and away from us. We hadn't even met her fiancé yet, nor did we know what he looked like either. Karter had really started getting into black history and was on this 'I'm black and I'm proud' shit. Every single time we spoke to her she was preaching about the color of the race and how we can't let the white man define who we are so most of the time we just let her do her… still would've been nice to see her though.

"Nope, she's been complaining about her back and shit

but she wants us to Face Time her when LeLe gets home." She responded as she worked hard on the arch. "I don't know why we gotta do all of this anyway. We could've had a simple dinner and that's it but noooo just like school days LeLe gets all the extra shit."

Just like this bitch to always be complaining. Probably why she couldn't keep a nigga. "You always complaining Kim… I'll be glad when you realize everything isn't about you. It's bad enough you barely wanted to send her letters and shit now you complaining about this?"

"It's not like I didn't want to though, I'm just not good with shit like this. You know I love that damn girl. At least I sent money for her books every other month." She plastered a smile on her face.

I curved the corner of my lips. "Um hmmm." I turned my attention to a chime from the door letting us know someone had entered or was heading out. Much to my surprise a fine ass nigga wearing a sharp royal blue pin striped and white suit walked in. Standing at about 6'1 maybe 220 in weight, he looked like a gentle giant with his light brown skin and dimples. He wore his thick hair in a low brush cut with waves. His beard was trimmed perfectly too. He didn't wear any jewelry like that but on his wrist he wore a shining Cartier watch. He smelled like money too. I watched Latrell clap him up, not like he knew him like that but just very cordial.

I specifically put a damn sign on the door that said 'CLOSED' and yet niggas were still walking in. I didn't give a damn if it wasn't my establishment. I had paid damn good money to rent it out and nobody was gonna just be barging in here. I didn't care how fine a nigga or his old ass daddy was. "I'm sorry…" I politely smiled. "It's a big sign on the door that says closed tonight." I told him until I was standing right in front of him.

He didn't even budge. Instead, he looked at me from head to toe checking me out. "Not bad…" He smiled. "Not bad at all."

I sucked my teeth and shift my weight from one leg to the other. "Look, you gotta go okay? I'm not trying to be rude but I promised the owners nobody was gone be in here."

"I'm glad you pay attention." He reached out his hand to shake mine. "I'm Cass…the owner… my man Trey rented it out to you with my approval." He looked around at the decorations. "I like how ya'll laid the place out; shit looking nice."

I was too embarrassed that I had tried to put down on the man who was responsible for this place. "OMG…" I shook my head as I chuckled and extended my hand to his. "I'm so sorry." I looked at him again. Made sense. This nigga looked like a corporate thug.

"It's cool…" He raised a brow. "Abbey right?"

"Yes… it's Abbey. Nice to meet you Cass… I love this place. It's so damn nice and the food… omgggg so bomb."

"Nice to meet you too ma…" He gave me a slight smile looking down at me since he was way taller anyway. "You responsible for the decorations ma?"

I shook my head and pointed to Kim instead. "Un un… my girl over there does all this shit… she's bad too. You should get her card." I suggested.

"Definitely need that…" He told me. I was so caught up talking to him; I didn't even notice the big ass bodyguards or whoever the hell they were standing at the door and obviously had come in with him. He looked like money and all but I'm not sure why he needed those big ass niggas with him. "I'mma get it on my way to the kitchen…" he told me. "Don't let me interrupt, ya'll do ya'll thing. I just stop by to pick up some paperwork." He told me before walking off heading over to Kim. I peeped her checking him out and laughed. This time; I couldn't even blame her for drooling over buddy. The nigga was fine.

* * *

IT DIDN'T TAKE MUCH LONGER to decorate and get everything set after that and now I was glad to be home. I had purchased my first house in North Miami a little over three months ago and loved being home. Most of the time I was searching through home décor magazines and shit since I enjoyed putting my spot together. I took a warm bath and slipped on a soft pink fleece suit with some low ankle socks so I could just slip on my shoes when I was ready. LeLe was being released at 4am and it was just a little after midnight.

I didn't want to fall asleep in fear that I may not hear my alarm to get up so I went and sat out on my porch and rolled me a joint watching the cars ride by since the Miami streets never slept anyway. I could walk out of my house any time of day, night, or wee hours of the morning and cars would be out. I had my favorite glass of Sweet Stella Rose Wine sitting next to me while I rolled a joint to smoke and ease my mind. Although LeLe had been gone 2 ½ years; a lot of shit had changed and I hoped she adjusted okay being that she was starting completely over. I pulled softly on the joint and exhaled making a smoke circle as it left my mouth. I was almost done when the black Challenger pulled up in my front yard turning the lights off before he hopped out.

"Bout time you made your way over here…" I licked my lips. "You done playing with them young hoes?" I asked like I was so much older than him. I'm a fresh 25 and although he is 21… I'm still older.

Trell had his dreads hanging down the side of his face. He was wearing a simple white tee and some Tru's. He smelled like he was fresh out the shower too just like I liked it. The aroma of weed and cologne filled the air. Ignoring my snide comment, he picked up the remainder of my wine and took it to the head. "I saw you sweating that nigga at the hookah lounge earlier. Don't get fucked up." He scooped me up off the porch walking me in the house. I loved doing shit like that to get on his nerves. This little thing we had started a little after LeLe went away.

It wasn't supposed to happen, it just did. He knew I missed my partner in crime. At first him and Leon used to come check me but then Leon got a bitch and just got missing and started doing his own thing that's why he's never around now. Meanwhile, Trell was still coming. Whether it was to get food if I cooked, or ask me for some advice, or just simply roll up and smoke not saying shit to each other at all. Eventually though, one thing led to another and now here we were still fucking in private and acting like we couldn't stand each other in public. LeLe didn't know shit about this and I didn't plan on her finding out either. We both kinda agreed to that.

As soon as the front door was closed and locked, we were at each other. Trell kissed me hard on the lips with my back pinned up against the wall and legs wrapped around his waist. I could feel the moistness in between my legs as my panties creamed anticipating him filling me up with his thick, juicy dick. "Mmmm" I moaned arching my back feeling the warmth of his tongue slithering the side of my neck. Inching his hands up to my waist, he pulled my pants down leg by leg while still holding me up with his strong arms.

Plunging two of his fingers inside of me he played in my honey pot inching his fingers in and out before removing them and sucking my juices off his fingers. "Damn that pussy taste good ma." He groaned licking his lips.

Trell held me by the ass as he used one hand to remove his dick before filling me up. "Oooohhhh." I gasped as soon as he entered me allowing me to place both my hands on his shoulders to bounce on the dick while he gripped my ass. I made sure my legs were still wrapped around him even tighter to keep my balance as we fucked on each other like some dogs in heat. "You.. know.. the… ohhhhhh…." I licked my lips squeezing my eyes. "You… know… the routine Trell… don't nut in meeee!" I cried in pleasure listening to the sounds of our skin smacking against one another mixed with the gushy sounds of our juices.

"Yeah… aiight." He growled pumping in me ferociously. Popping a titty from out of my bra; he used his tongue circling my hard nipple before placing it in his mouth where he gently sucked.

"Ohhh my Godddddd!" I bucked filling my body heating up. Trell penetrated me harder and harder. With each stroke I felt his dick become more swollen.

"I'm bout to nut ma…" He pumped. "Oh shitttt." Closing his eyes. He let go of his warm nut all in my walls as my pussy contracted allowing me to have a hard orgasm right along with him.

"Fuckkkk!" I yelled out in pleasure. Hugging him tight with both arms wrapped around his neck. I felt his knees buck a little but he didn't drop me. Instead he walked me over to the couch where we both flopped down trying to catch our breath. "You better go get me a plan B in the morning."

He nodded his head. "I gotchu."

After we cleaned ourselves up. We ended up in my bed going for round two until we fell asleep. I loved watching Trell sleep cause he looked so fine and peaceful. Truth is, I really liked his ass but there was no way I could tell him that cause I knew this couldn't go any further than what it was now. I placed a kiss on his lips and laid on his chest just listening to his heart. "I like your lil young ass… but this shit could never go anywhere." I whispered before closing my eyes.

An hour later my alarm was going off. "Trell, wake up." I told him. "It's time to go get LeLe. Is Mrs. Latia going?" I asked about his mama.

He woke up rubbing the sleep from his eyes. "Nah, told her don't come out this late. Gotta pick up Leon and we going." He stood up putting his shit on. "You can ride with us." He suggested.

I got up to put my clothes back on as well. "Umm no… how that's gone look me showing up with ya'll?"

He frowned. "No kinda way, the fuck you mean? You act like she gone know we fucking cause we showed up together. You gotta chill ma." He was now putting on his shoes. "Time ticking, you either coming or going. If not drive ya own car but that shit makes no sense." He shrugged.

Trell was right. I needed to chill the fuck out. I got dressed and put my own shoes on. "Cool… I'll ride with ya'll under one condition."

He finally looked up with those deep brown eyes and long lashes. "What?"

"Stop down the street to the 24-hour Walgreens and get my damn Plan B." I told him before grabbing my keys, and setting the alarm. Next, we walked out the house and got in his car. I think we both could agree there was no argument here.

LEANDRA 'LELE' WELLS

"WELLS! LET'S GO!" C.O Richardson yelled. The words I'd waited 2 ½ years to hear. I remember the first day coming in this shit; and the time to leave seemed so far-fetched. I spent every hour I could on my bunk in my feelings while all my friends were graduating college, starting careers, buying houses, party decorators… shit even Karter was engaged and married living in a big ass house. Now here I was about to come home to not shit. Not a pot to piss in nor a window to throw it out. Word up, I felt like the lowest bum bitch of all times.

Walking down the cold halls had my feet feeling heavy as shit cause what was supposed to be happy had been so bitter-sweet. One thing I can say is the whole experience made me a different person. I came in trying to be everybody's friend; BIG MISTAKE! Me doing just that is what made me have multiple fights trying to defend myself and defend my pussy cause them big ole dyke hoes sho tried to take it. After that, I spent most of my time in the library and in the kitchen cooking after I stayed out of trouble and was granted privileges for good behavior.

Richardson looked out for me though; he kept me on my toes and whenever I was feeling down or just wanted to hurt some fucking body, he gave me one of his good ole pep talks and I'd get back right. I tried to call everybody at least a couple times out the month but truth be told. I hated calling home cause that shit made me sad and depressed as fuck. I just wanted to do my time and get home. "They gave me probation for the remainder of my time Richardson." I told him as he walked me to property to get my belongings." He stood a little taller than me and had salt and pepper hair that he always kept low. His dark skin showed his muscles and although in his late 40's he looked really good and always spoke highly of his wife and grown children. Two boys and a girl, which he'd sent off to college. Underneath being a good father, husband, and correction officer; he's hood as fuck and always kept it real.

"It's gon' be okay Wells… you got this. You just remember don't let none of these trick ass bitches and no good niggas trick you outta your spot. You always put you first. Remember that and you'll be okay. I've watched you all this time beat the odds." He paused and gave me a nod of the head. "You something special. This aint no place for you. You make peace with your situation and get back out there and do what you gotta do."

"I got you Rich… thanks for everything." I smiled before walking into property. After that, I was walked out and through those gates clutching my brown bag. The weather in the wee hours of the morning was kinda nippy and dark as hell but a big ass smile spread across my face when I saw Abbey, Leon, and Latrell waiting on me posted up on top of a black on black Challenger. I took off as fast as I could with tears cascading down my face. I hadn't felt this adrenaline a few minutes ago but being beyond custody now had me feeling some type of way.

"LeLe!!!!" Abbey hugged me first damn near pushing my fine ass brothers out of the way.

"Damn Abbey…" Leon shook his head frowning at her. Something looked different with him. He didn't rock the baggy jeans look. He rocked a pair of skinny jeans, some black and white vans and a Graphic tee. Latrell looked the same that I remembered; on his hood shit with his now super long dreads. I wasn't expecting Abbey to be with them but I'm glad they all made it to come get me.

After we all hugged, I got in the back seat of the car with Abbey while Latrell and Leon sat in the front. "OMG ya'll I need a damn big mac, some fries, shit… something… anything. I need another reminder that I'm no longer property of the state."

They all laughed and talk shit but Leon had Trell take me to Denny's instead where I ordered one big ass cheeseburger, fries, some French toast, scrambled eggs, sausage, bacon, ham, and hash browns. My eyes lit up with all of the food in front of me. The rest of them ordered one thing on the menu but let me have whatever I liked. I knew I couldn't eat it all, but it damn sure didn't hurt to taste everything. All the slop we get fed behind bars… I was surprised I had gained any weight, which went straight to my ass and thighs.

"Slow the fuck down LeLe… that food ain't going nowhere." Trell laughed so hard he was holding his stomach. "Bad enough yo ass out here looking like one of those bitches from the color purple the way you got your hair braided back. We gotta get that done asap."

I stopped chewing. Abbey elbowed him hard as fuck. "Ouch!" He groaned. "What I do?" He looked confused.

"Leave her alone." Abbey warned.

I laughed at them both. "My shit is kinda fucked up…" I shrugged.

Latrell was still eyeing Abbey as he munched on his pancakes. "What I tell you bout putting yo hands on me?"

She rolled her eyes. "Oh please…"

Leon wasn't even looking up. "Ya'll argue and fight more than James and Florida…" He was all in his phone texting somebody. "Sick of ya'll muhfuckas." He said under his breath.

"You know, for somebody who never says shit at all, that's a whole lot for you to be saying right now. Besides, this nigga get on my nerves." Abbey dug into her bag and popped some type of pill in her mouth before gulping it down.

"Yeah right… you love me." Trell said as he picked up his ringing phone and ignored a call.

"Nigga please." She sassed.

"Abbey what kinda pill you just took?" I asked mostly out of concern cause I'd never seen her take anything. She's one of those people refused to take a cold tablet when she wasn't feeling well. "Everything okay with you?"

She nodded her head. "Yep… just a little antibiotic." She stabbed her pancake chewing on it.

I shrugged and paid attention to Leon. "I like your new look… you don't look all thuggish no more."

"Yeah but the bitches still love that nigga…" Latrell said.

Leon sucked his teeth. "Man, fuck them bitches." Just then a Face time call was coming through on his phone from 'bae' and he walked away to answer it.

Latrell watched. "Nigga been so secretive lately. Think somebody wanna steal his hoes."

Abbey elbowed him again and the arguing started all over again. I could truly say my damn stomach hurt from laughing at them. It was like watching my siblings argue cause that's just how they acted. My stomach hurt so damn bad after munching down half of my food but it felt damn good being home. I swore upon God that I would never do shit else to jeopardize my freedom. I didn't give a damn, that shit was simply not worth it.

LEANDRA 'LELE' WELLS

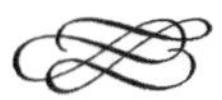

"You look to the fuck good! Like bitchhhhh. Un Un don't play with my friend!" Abbey walked around me checking me out. I didn't wanna tell her I wasn't feeling this going out shit but she insisted that I had to go cause she wasn't letting me miss my 'Welcome Home' party. I especially didn't like feeling like shit had to be done for me. She wanted me all dressed up so she got me this bad ass Armani dress that stopped right before my knees but yet hugged every inch of my body; in my opinion just showing way too much. The matching Red Bottoms were already killing my feet too. She had a girl she knows come give me a soft beat on the face and even paid for me to get my hair washed, treated, and styled in a layered bob with the part down the middle. I wasn't too happy about trimming my hair but it was much needed.

"I swear I'mma pay you back soon as I come up." I told her.

She waved me off. "No the fuck you not... what are friends for?"

I could've paid for this shit with the money my brothers

had given me, which was only 500 a piece, but I needed to try to hold on to it until I could figure out what I wanted to do with myself. After about another hour, we were headed out. Abbey was rolling in a clean ass all white ML350 Benz that had the peanut butter guts on the inside. Made me happy she was doing damn good. "I need to see a smile on your face." She told me. "You need to loosen up. Want a drink? Some dick? What?"

"Nah…" I chuckled. "Ion drink no more Abbey… I decided that shit long time ago. Ion smoke no more either; well… actually that's not by choice but I can't afford to fail a drug test and take a chance on being violated. Matter fact, ion wanna be round nobody that's smoking so I hope that's all gone be in this Hookah lounge is Hookahs… cause bitch… if niggas gone be smoking take me the fuck back to my mama house." I ranted panicking just thinking about going back. "And you know what? Some dick does sound good but that's all a nigga can give me is some dick cause I don't have time to be falling in love with nobody. I don't have shit to give to myself let alone bring something to the table for a nigga."

"Damnnnn… relax." She held up a hand pulling in the parking lot.

"Looks like a whole bunch of cars out to me." I sunk down lower in the seat.

"Girl!" She fell out laughing. "Nobody can see you behind the dark ass tints ion know what you hiding for."

It took 15 minutes for me to get over my anxiety of being around a bunch of people. What triggered me the most was the fact that I didn't wanna be looked at or labeled as a murderer. That's how people would do you. Be in your face and talk about you like a dog later.

We had to bump through a whole bunch of people who were the friends of other people that decided to just tag along before we could even get to our section. Kim was running around making sure everybody was okay but when she saw me she stopped what she was doing and put the bottle down. "Bout time they let my bitch out!" She squealed in excitement as we embraced each other. I eyed her down cause she look too damn good herself. I knew she was probably still the same little hater deep down inside but she did keep it real and kept money and shit on my books every other month or when she could.

"Kimmm… wussup girl. You hooked this place up tonight. Feels good to be back!" I yelled over the music. As bad as I was trying to act normal, I just felt so out of place around all these people but I didn't wanna complain and seem ungrateful. While they were here to celebrate me; the only thing I could focus on was where my next dollar was coming from and rightfully so. Not to mention getting a job since I'm now a convicted felon.

Kim hugged me tightly but already seemed like she was half drunk. "Yesss… I do my thing boo. I'm so happy you home. it's only up from here." She slurred holding her half bottle of Remy in the air doing an invisible toast. "Where's your drink?"

I shook my head and smiled. "Ion drink no more… I'm done with that shit."

Abbey yawned seeming real uninterested in my last statement but I didn't have time to dwell on that. The whole place was a vibe. The DJ started spinning Wale's new song 'On Chill' which I'd heard in jail too many times and loved this song so much. I closed my eyes and started moving my hips like I was the only one in the club while singing along:

We've been on the tragedy for months,
Why can't you agree with me for once?
Maybe we can be on chill tonight,

Maybe I can give you chills too.
We've been on the tragedy for months,
Why can't you agree with me for once?
Maybe we can be on chill tonight,
Maybe I can give you chills too.

When I opened my eyes it was multiple niggas staring at me but one that got my attention, looked like he was looking right through me. Feeling exposed I took a seat and sipped my water trying to ignore him burning a hole through me. I tried to play it cool like I didn't see him while praying his ass didn't walk over to me. My heart was still broken and I just didn't have time to give it to nan other niggas. At this rate, my heart just couldn't be saved so I didn't need for nobody to try it. Underneath this dress, makeup and everything else around me; I was still fucking sad.

"I know you see that fine as nigga looking at you…"

I didn't even realize Abbey had been watching me. "Yeah, who the fuck is that?"

"That's Trey… he's like the right-hand man of the dude who own this spot… nigga name Cass and he's fine as hell too."

Trey was tall and medium built. Even from where we stood, the waves in his thick black hair could be seen bouncing from the lights above. I'd say he had to be about 6 feet and every time he opened his mouth I could see he had a mouth full of gold teeth. His skin was as dark as midnight but his facial features were very handsome. He was wearing black slacks with a long sleeve collard button down. Just looked like he was chilling, nothing flashy outside of that besides the icy chain he wore around his neck.

I frowned. "Why he looking so damn mean? And why he walking over here?" I asked. "You gave him some play?"

She shook her head. "Nope." Sipping her Remy and red bull she acted like it was nothing.

As soon as he walked over the first thing I smelled was the freshness of his cologne. "Come with me…" he told me still not breaking his glare.

Abbey cleared her throat. "Nigga she aint goin' nowhere with you… we don't even know you… I mean, you hooked me up with the spot and all but that aint come with no free dates or no shit like that."

Trey gave Abbey one look. If I could call it… it was that 'shut the fuck up' look… but still he didn't address her. He addressed me instead. "I look like a nigga that gotta take some pussy? Come with me, Cass wanted to personally welcome you home…" He looked me up and down. "I'm not asking either… come on." His voice was so demanding and yet intriguing. I could tell he was the type of nigga that didn't play no games.

"I'll be right back Abbey… I'm a big girl. I can at least speak to the man and thank him." I told her. She wasn't feeling it but she nod her head agreeing while watching us both like a hawk as I followed him bumping through people. Since he was a few steps ahead of me, I kept getting lost in the crowd or by niggas stopping me. I assume Trey must've been irritated with me for my lack of not being able to keep up, which prompted him to reach back and grab my hand so he can lead the way.

It had been so long since I touched a man and the feeling of his strong hand grabbing mine felt damn good. When we finally made it to the section he was leading me to, he dropped my hand like a hot cake and went and took a seat in the section. I was surprised to see Kim sitting on the lap of a good-looking dude. Looked like a corporate thug if you asked me. The way he was just laid back with not a care in the world told me he must've been the person asking for me.

These damn red Bottoms were killing my feet. I didn't see how women did this shit; I don't care how good these damn heels look they are horrible! I could barely stand straight at this point and was ready to get this meet and greet over with. He casually gave Kim a light tap on the ass and whispered something in her ear prompting her to get up. "Hey girl… be right back." She said all cheery. It was like she was sober all-of-a-sudden.

The nigga Cass was looking me up and down right along with the rest of the crew. "Damn, shawty ain't tell me you was this bad." He looked at me in the eyes as he extended one hand to shake mine. "I'm Cass ma… I wanted to personally welcome you home. I don't know what you did to be locked up like an animal but take it from a nigga who been there, it's much sweeter on this side."

I nod my head in agreement as I shook his hand back. "I appreciate that…"

"What you drinking? You can have whatever you like. It's on me. You and yo girls need to enjoy. You deserve that."

"I don't deserve anything of this…" I replied under my breath and then spoke up. "Thank you, but ion drink no more. That shit ain't for me."

He sat back in the chair and licked his lips. "I like that…"

"Yeah… me too." I was now ready to go. "Thanks though Cass. I appreciate you for letting my girl rent out the spot and for letting my other girl decorate… it's so nice in here." I smiled.

"You taste the food yet?" He cooley asked.

I shook my head. "Not yet but I'm bout to go try some now. Heard all about it."

He smiled. "Yeah, you do that, and let me know what you think."

"Will do." I agreed and extended my hand to his again. "Well, it was nice meeting you but imma get back on my side."

Without another word, he acknowledged that with a simple nod of the head while he popped an open a bottle of Belaire. I wanted to thank Trey for walking me over but he wasn't paying my ass no mind. Instead he was examining everything in the place but me. He didn't have a bunch of hoes in his face, nor did he care to entertain none of the niggas either. He seemed so… mysterious to me.

"So what happen?" Abbey asked as soon as I got back. I shrugged and sat down.

"Shit, nothing… he really did just wanna welcome me home. That's it." We both looked back over in that direction of where Cass was sitting while I explained to Abbey our short introduction encounter when something, or should I say somebody caught my eye. Clapping it up and talking with the same nigga I'd just met. "Wait… is that…" I pointed and squint my eyes. My heart raced a bit cause he was looking just like Malik.

"Yep… that's Majestic's ass." She confirmed. "Scary huh?"

He must've felt me staring cause he locked eyes with me. "Too damn scary."

I had a good time… but now… I was ready to go.

LEANDRA 'LELE' WELLS

My head was pounding the following morning since Abbey had me out all damn night. "LeLe wake up!" My mama yelled in my room as she stood at the door. "I got a newspaper out here on the table with breakfast. I can't let you come home and get comfortable or feel sorry for yourself… you need to get a job baby."

"Newspaper?" I mumbled under the covers wishing she would go the fuck away. I wasn't even sleep. I was up with the damn chickens. Being in prison had my body adjusted to get up super early; I wasn't tired my head just hurt but to keep her content; I just got up. "I don't need a newspaper. That's why they have Wi-Fi and computers and stuff ma."

"I don't keep none of that shit in this house just another reason to spend money so you gone have to look at this paper or go down to the library and use all they gadgets." She laughed before walking out.

I went ahead and got my ass up. Walking across the hall to the shower and not having to share with a bunch of other bitches was such a privilege that I enjoyed the hot water tickling my skin for the first ten minutes and then scrubbed before the water got cold. The only clothes I had were my old clothes that I could barely fit now so I rummaged through everything until I found some tight fitted jeans and a white tight fitted Guess shirt that hugged my breast. I had a crisp pair of all white Nike Airmax still in the box so I put them on and lotion down my soft, toned skin.

Since my hair was still intact I didn't have to do much besides run my fingers through it. Next, I went to the drawer where I had my money and peeled off two twenty-dollar bills and stuffed them in the back of my jeans pocket. My mama was at the table eating some scrambled eggs and bacon but I wasn't in the mood to eat so I grabbed one piece of bacon and popped it in my mouth. "I'll be back ma… I'mma walk to the Library…"

"You don't wanna drive your car?" She asked. I shook my head no. I wasn't ready to get behind the wheel. My old car had been sitting in her yard all this time and I didn't plan on touching it now. "Well, you at least don't want me to take you? Girl it's hotter than fish grease out there today… you'll fasho have a heat stroke."

I chuckled. "I'm good ma… I'll be back." When I opened the door, it was really hot as fuck but I'd had plenty hot days on the yard so I ignored it and started my journey for the next four blocks. Halfway to the Library and I wished I'd took that ride from her cause a bitch was hot. Sweat dripped from my forehead. Had me fanning myself with one hand which wasn't doing any justice.

I was all prepared to mind my business when a matte black G-Wagon pulled up on the side of me. I didn't stop. I kept walking. I wasn't worried about nobody fucking with me cause I'd learned how to fight real good in prison. "Now you know it's too hot and you too damn fine to be out here walking like this ma…" A familiar voice boomed from the side of me. The same nigga from last night, Cass… was rolling on the side of me while drinking a Heineken. "Where you going? I'll take you… and what nigga got you out here walking anyway?" He asked.

I didn't stop, I kept going while paying his fine ass no mind cause I didn't have time for this. My clothes were starting to stick to my body and I needed to get out of this heat. "I'm fine… I'm almost where I'm going." I told him using my hand to shield the sun from my eyes.

"It don't matter ma… it's too fuckin' hot. I can't let you be out here in this heat like this while I'm in this icebox sippin' on Heinekens and shit… Get in… either that, or I'll just have to follow you getting on yo fucking nerves all the way to yo destination."

As bad as I didn't want to I had to laugh imagining that.

"Ahhh she smiles…" He chuckled. "Pretty ass smile too. Come on shawty, I'll take you. Nigga ain't no rapist or no shit like that. You better off in here with me rather than a pervert snatch yo ass up. You know this sex trafficking shit wild out here now…" He made a valid point.

I thought about what he said and gave in… not because I really wanted to, but because I was burning the fuck up. "Aiight I'll let you take me." I agreed. "But one second." I ran to the back of his fancy truck and snapped a picture of his license plates. Quickly I sent it to Abbey and let her know if anything happens to me… give the police this plate number.

As soon as I got in Cass was looking at me crazy. "Yo I ain't gone do nothing to you ma."

I allowed myself to sink in his soft leather seat and put the air directly on me. I immediately felt better. "Oh I know… I gave my girl your tag number just in case."

Cass lightly chuckled and pulled off. "So where too lil mama?"

I pointed straight ahead. "To the library… and it's Leandra but everybody calls me LeLe." I corrected him. I wasn't his girl for him to be giving me nicknames.

He took a swig from his beer and then tossed the bottle out in the road causing it to shatter. "My bad Ms. LeLe…" He threw his hands up. "Can I ask what's at the library?"

I didn't mind telling him, hell, it was all a part of my testimony. "I need to go look for a job and the shit is frustrating cause I know don't nobody wanna hire a convicted felon." I sighed.

He didn't even budge or change his demeanor when I said that. I know this cause I was observing for that. "Yeah, I know all about that." He turned the corner and pulled in front of the Library putting the car in park. "Looks can be deceiving ma… you don't look like you got it in you to be a part of no criminal activity so what you do?" He stared at me. "What? Grand theft or some shit?"

"Nah…" I said under my breath. "And honestly I'm not ready to talk about it. I took a deep breath and shook thoughts of the accident out of my head. "Thanks for the ride though; I appreciate that."

"What time you wanna leave?"

I frowned. "Why?"

"So I can pick you back up…" He replied like that was a no brainer.

"I didn't ask for a ride back."

"You aint got to… I told you… it's crazy people out here. I'll come get you."

I nibbled on my bottom lip out of habit while I thought about it. It didn't take long. I didn't wanna get snatched the fuck up. "I need about three hours…"

He nod his head while still staring at me. "Aiight…. Cool. I'll be back."

When he pulled off, I stared at his truck until I could no longer see it in my sight before walking into the library and getting to work. It took damn near an hour for me to put together my resume and another two hours of searching, but I was tired as hell. The people were dwindling away little by little, which left only me. I wasn't sure if the librarian was ready to go to lunch or get off the clock but I felt like she was rushing me every time she would come over and ask if I needed assistance. "Look lady… if I need you. I'll call you over. Don't you come back over here disturbing me." I sassed. She scurried away. This shit was harder than I thought. Every single job wanted you to be bilingual and also made it very clear a background check would be involved. Shit had me mad tight.

I already knew none of these jobs were going to hire me but it didn't hurt to try, so I still submitted my resume to as many jobs as I could. I was exhausted as hell after that and really didn't feel like walking home but as soon as I made it outside… Cass was backed in with the windows down smoking a joint. "Come on… you gone stand there or we gotta go through this all over again?"

"I'm not getting in that damn truck with you smoking that shit. I don't want no secondhand smoke or none of that shit in my system. Matter fact, I'm not even getting in that truck with it smelling like weed. You get pulled over; my black ass gets violated." I pivoted around clutching the resumes I had in my hand to take home with me. Without another word I was beating the pavement. From behind me, I heard the door slam and the sound of him hitting the lock button.

"Aye hold up!" He ran behind me until he caught up. "Damn you tough…"

"I just refuse to go back… you ever been to prison?" I asked still walking.

"Hell yeah… and I ain't goin' back either. Them muhfuckas gone have to kill me first cause I'm not ever goin' back." He said in all seriousness. I briefly looked at him. He looked just as good in his street clothes than he did in his dressy clothes like last night.

"Well… you feel me then." I said. "I can't afford to be around nothing or nobody that's gone jeopardize my freedom to that extent. I don't want to be around nobody while they smoking, neither do I wanna be around nobody involved in criminal activity either."

"Well you aint gotta worry about that ma… I'm a businessman; I do smoke, but I promise I won't do it around you." He gave me a sexy little smile. I hated the fact that I was actually enjoying his company.

I furrowed my brows. "Who said I planned on being around you after this?"

Popping his imaginary collar, he told me. "Oh… you will… trust me." I bust out laughing at that remark. His cocky ass attitude was definitely on one thousand. "How did the job search go?" He asked.

"I already know they ain't gone call me back but I did some anyway. In prison I learned how to cook real good. Maybe I can apply at a cooking job. I actually love cooking now and trying new things. I mean, I went to school for business management too, but I didn't finish cause I got locked up."

"Well see, you should've mentioned this earlier. If you want a cooking job I can handle that for you. You can work for me at Jazzy's Hookah Lounge."

My eyes lit up. "Really???" Then as quick as they lit up I was squinting at him. "Why you being so nice? What's the catch?"

"Ain't no catch ma… I'm just tryna help a young sister

out. I done been on the other side of them gates before so I know how shit is. You want the job or not?"

"But you don't even know if my cooking is good…"

"Yeah, I know… that's why you gone cook for me this weekend. I'll pick you up Saturday at bout 5… be ready." I couldn't do nothing but shake my head. "And come with a different attitude… you savage but under all that I know you a good person."

I turned my nose up. "Savage?"

"Yeah… like this hot ass sun out here you got me sweating in… done walked yo ass damn near home. Be ready!"

I watched him jog all the way back down the block until he was out of sight trying to ignore the little butterflies I had. I almost called him back to give him my number wondering how I was going to show him that I could cook if he didn't even know how to contact me. I decided against it though… something told me that wouldn't even be an issued. He'd find me.

LEON WELLS

"Come over here bae…." Kevin pat the spot on the bed next to him. I hadn't even realized I was staring off into space. Hiding this part of my life had me all fucked up and twisted. Had me even more fucked up cause I was hiding it from both LeLe and Latrell. The old me would've never hid shit from them. Our parents… yeah that's one thing but from each other… nah wasn't too fond of that.

I stood at the window with my shirt off and basketball shorts on. I was supposed to be heading to practice at the school in a lil bit but today… my mood was all off. I just didn't feel like going. "Hol up…" I told him. "I'm coming."

Figuring out what the fuck I was constantly doing here was an everyday battle as I struggled with my sexuality. I had always been attracted to girls and fucked a lot of them too. To my knowledge I'd never been attracted to a man… until I met Kevin almost a year ago. He's a student at UM just like me and Trell. This shit was killing me. A nigga that looked like me wasn't supposed to be doing this shit, at the same time I couldn't help what I felt. I thanked Kevin over and over for being patient with me, but I could tell the stress was getting to him sometimes of constantly having to be hidden; for example… me walking right pass him in the halls like he didn't even exist.

I'm the star on the basketball team. I'm not no soft ass nigga, ain't no pushover… and was raised well. I didn't even know what this meant. What I did know is nobody could find out about this secret I'd been hiding… especially not Trell. I never expected myself to be goin' out like this. I honestly don't even know how it led to this shit but it did and now a nigga was in too deep. I wasn't even craving females no more. Maybe I never really wasn't in the first place; was probably just doing that shit cause pussy was being thrown left and right and I knew I could do it. That and I also had an image to keep up with.

I resented Kevin like a muthafucka some days. I felt like a bitch, like he turned me out. Sometimes, I wanted to punch him in his shit. Other days, I wanted to love him just as hard as he loved me. Shit was just tough. Deep in my thoughts, I felt Kevin come behind me rubbing my bare shoulders…I didn't stop him.

"Why you so stressed out? Something happened that you didn't tell me about? Somebody find out about me? What?" His voice was full of concern but Kevin is just like that. If he gave a fuck about you, then he'd do anything to fix you if you were down. Give a nigga his last penny, or the shirt off his back and he was like that with family too. One would think he'd be a stuck-up ass brat since he came from money and all with his daddy being a lawyer and his mama being a judge but it wasn't like that.

When I first saw Kevin, I was attracted to his light green eyes, almost cat like. He wore his hair braided back in corn rolls and stood about 5'5. His body was toned being that he ran cross-country track all of life. I could honestly say he's one of the prettiest niggas I'd ever seen. Being around him, I could be one way. I ain't have no worries, or none of that shit but being away from him, I had to be a different person. I had to maintain the street nigga mentality that I'd grew up around or else niggas would try me.

"I'm cool… just thinking." I told him.

"Is it somebody else?" He asked worried.

I shook my head. "Nah…"

"Is it the fact that you still hiding me?"

I sucked my teeth and removed his hands from my shoulders. "Maybe…" I replied agitated. "Shit ion know… this shit ain't easy."

Kevin walked around to the front of me so he could look me in the face. Although nice; he wasn't a push over at all. He wasn't one of the feminine type of gay dudes either. He didn't try to speak with an extra high-pitched voice or go all out his way to be super flamboyant and shit. He was just… regular. Not a thug or no shit like that but just super pretty and loved nice shit. He was always himself and never tried to detour from that. Sometimes I was jealous of the way he gave no fucks about who he really was.

"You know… you can't be real with other people around you until you're real with yourself first Leon. You don't think it bothers me how you walk right pass me in the halls? Or how you only show affection or speak to me if it's behind these walls? How do you think I feel telling you that I love you only for you to never say it back?" He asked with seriousness on his face. "I know who I am… you need to figure out who you are."

"You want me to just be round this muthafucka openly admitting that I'm gay…" I shook my head and put my shoes on cause I knew he was about to be on his bullshit.

He stood over me. "But you are gay Leon… no matter how you try to word it."

"Nigga… I ain't gay." I mumbled under my breath now looking for my phone.

He threw his arms up and walked away talking shit. "Right, so I guess your dick just slipped in my asshole on mistake so many times I can't even fucking count."

I hopped up and rushed his ass ready to choke the shit out of him for saying that shit. "Say that shit again!" I growled.

He grabbed his flower vase that sat by his room door and picked it up. "Or else what! Nigga, I wish you would! This vase will be eating the whole right side of your face up."

This fighting shit wasn't new for us. Kevin was my headache and my peace a lot of times but when we fought… we fought. Mostly because we both were always caught up in our own emotions.

"You know what yo… I'm not even finna do this shit with you today. I'm bout to bounce. I'll see you when I see you." I grabbed my keys and walk past him still holding the vase giving me the 'I don't give a fuck look.'

"You're so fucking selfish." He rambled off. "That's all you do is run and hide… hide your life… your sexuality, your true feelings for me! Just admit the shit, you love me."

He was now walking behind me talking his shit… and it took every fucking thing in me for me not to swing on his ass knowing as soon as I did that, we were bout to tear this whole fucking apartment up. I could easily beat Kevin cause he ain't no damn fighter like that. He just talked a lot of shit… but it wasn't no need cause I knew eventually; my black ass would stay away for a little bit and then be right back.

I didn't even look behind me when I slammed the door walking out. Nor did I look when I heard the door locking behind me. However, it did bother me to watch him watching me pull off from his living room window with tears in his eyes. I felt bad as fuck… I wasn't tryna hurt him… he's human and had feelings just like everybody else did. I wasn't about to go apologize though cause truth is… it's not his fault. This shit is all on me.

Originally I wasn't going to practice, but I needed to blow off some steam and frustration so I went ahead and did that on the court. When it was time to go, Trell was in the parking lot macking with a cute lil butterscotch honey. I assume he was leaving football practice cause that's the only time he would be here late. Damn sho wasn't to study. "Wus good bro?" I clapped him up.

"Shit… can't call it… same ole." He shook his dreads lose.

"What the hell…" the chick he was talking to looked back and forth at us both. "I didn't know you had a twin. OMG ya'll look exactly alike outside of the hair."

I chuckled. "Yeah…"

Trell nod his head and licked his lips. "Yeah… but check this out… you make sure you pick up tonight when I call you."

I knew she was gone give him some pussy by the way she was lusting at the nigga. "You know I am… I have a cute roommate too… bring your brother." She walked off.

"Nope… nigga don't even ask… I gotta study ion got time to be fuckin' with no hoes."

Trell looked at me like I was crazy as fuck to be passing up some pussy. "You done got lame as fuck… where my brother at?" He used his finger tapping on my head. "Leon! Nigga you in there somewhere?"

Mushing his hand away I laughed. "Man get the fuck outta here…" I said. "I just ain't on that shit."

He fold his arms across his chest. "Yo ass done fell in

love that's all… shit I can't wait to meet her… you be hiding the bitch like we gone eat her up or something."

I clapped him up again avoiding the conversation like always. "Man whatever yo." I chuckled. "I'll see you at the spot tonight… Majestic still wanna meet?"

"Oh fasho…"

"Aiight… we gone get this money."

"Bet…" Trell replied before getting in his car. When he pulled off I walked to my car. Same exact Challenger as his only my shit is red. When I put my bags in the car I couldn't help but keep replaying his words in my head. Damn… was I in love?

ABBEY DANIELS

"Yes, you heard me right. I'm here to see Trey or Cass, whichever one about getting my deposit back." I preached to the girl working the front register at Jazzy's. "Are they here? I should've had my deposit mailed back to me by now but it's taking forever."

"Um ma'am… you can talk to Cass since he's here, but I mean… I'm sure you'd get your deposit as promised. Neither one of them are pressed for no money." The young girl sassed. Looked like she couldn't have been no older than seventeen or so and that's the only thing that stopped me from reaching across the counter and slapping her in her damn mouth for talking to me all crazy.

I lightly tapped my freshly manicured nails on the counter and gave her one more look. "I'mma let your lil young ass slide with your slick comment cause I'm not going to jail for somebody who still smells like piss. But since he's here I'll help myself." I politely smiled and walked around to the back. I didn't give a shit that she threatened to call the police on me. I didn't even know where I was going but I assumed his office had to be one of the closed doors in the hallway.

I was all prepared to open every door until I got the right one when a voice distracted me. "What the hell?" I mumbled following the voice to the kitchen where pots were clacking and rumbling. The smell instantly made my stomach growl. "It couldn't be…." I walked in staggering upon LeLe with an apron on stirring a huge pot of collard greens with smoked turkey. "LeLe?" I frowned causing her to jump. She looked as if she had been hard at work too. The sloppy bun she wore was under a hair net to keep the hair from falling in the food.

She gasped and then relaxed when she realized it was me. With a focused look on her face she went right back to work. "Girl, you scared the shit out of me. What you doing here?"

"Shit, I came to get my deposit back, what the hell you doing here and why you in this man kitchen cooking?" For the life of me I couldn't figure this shit out.

"Oh, yeah, since I used to cook in the prison and I'm having a hard time finding a job he offered me one cooking here. I don't mind either so don't you go talking your shit. I need some dough and I refuse to have anybody doing everything for me like I'm some bum ass bitch cause I'm not." She rambled on.

I didn't like the idea of her slaving in this hot ass kitchen, but knowing LeLe it wasn't shit I could say to change her mind when it was well made up about something; especially concerning her livelihood. I had to pierce my lips together on this one but I had a mouthful for Cass ass. "Ok fine… I won't… now where is Cass?"

She was so focused on the dishes she was cooking, she barely even looked at me. "Down the hall to the right."

I walked out as my heals echoed with every step that I took. Knocking on the door, I waited for a response, which it only took a second for the door to open up and I was greeted with two big ass niggas first. "Um excuse me…" I frowned.

"She good." Cass spoke from his desk while counting the money that was in front of him. "What's good ma?"

"My money sir… I'mma need somebody to run me that cause I never got my deposit back." I told him. "I know this isn't the way a businessman like you conducts business."

He stopped counting the money and leaned back in his chair after picking up the pre rolled joint so he could look at me. He lit it up. "You ain't scared to talk to me like that?"

"Are you gonna kill me?" I asked sarcastically.

"Do I look like a killer?"

"Is this some kinda trick question? No… you don't." I sighed.

He laughed. "Most of us don't…"

I swallowed hard. I don't know why but I could tell he was serious even with the laugh disguising it.

He must've peeped the concern on my face. "Chill ma… ain't nobody gone do shit to you but maybe we having some kinda communication issue cause ya girl Kim collected your deposit the same night. You and LeLe left early remember?"

I thought back to that night. We had indeed left early cause LeLe got shook when she spotted Majestic. She just wasn't ready to face him. I think the guilt was still too much for her so we did leave. He could be right but now I had to cuss Kim ass out for not telling me and for having me in here looking stupid. "Oh… guess she forgot to tell me that." I shook my head. "I'm sorry about that. No pun intended."

"None taken… ain't my character to steal from nobody shorty."

"Good… cause I wouldn't mind doing business with you again…"

He nod his head getting back to counting with the joint hanging from his mouth. His weed smelled so good. I couldn't wait to get home and roll my shit after a long day and I wouldn't dare ask him to hit his. I had a rule… if I didn't see them roll it, I wasn't smoking it. Period. No telling what kinda shit people put in the weed to get that extra lace now days. "Yeah, we can do that. Ya girl LeLe mean on them pots too. Had shorty make a couple of samples for me earlier today and she's been at it since. She really got a passion for that shit."

"Yeah… I guess she does." I mumbled cause I didn't know if she did or if she was just doing anything to get money. "Does my pretty ass friend look like she's supposed to be slaving in the kitchen though? She's smart… she's beautiful… she's intelligent as fuck."

"Look, she needed somewhere to start and I'm helping her… ain't like she's doing it for free… hell… I'm paying her enough." He said nonchalantly.

"I just wanna make sure she's not settling."

He furrowed his thick brows. "If you know ya friend like you say you do… she ain't settling. Matter fact, she's thorough as fuck. She'll find her way again."

The way he said that and the look on his face when he said it made me feel like he had more intentions for LeLe than what he was trying to make it seem like. As a friend, I knew I had to watch his ass cause I didn't want nobody to think they could take advantage of her. I nod my head and agreed with him instead. "Okay, as long as it's genuine." I looked down at my watch. "I have to go but I'll see you around Cass. Make sure you take care of my girl when she's in your care."

"Trust me…. She's good." He told me. All three of them watched me as I walked out. I stopped back by the kitchen to tell LeLe I was about to go but she was already waiting for me with a carryout in her hand.

"Here girl… just a lil sum'n sum'n cause you know yo

ass can't cook and probably finna go buy something anyway." She laughed removing her headphones from her ears.

"Bitch please don't even do me like that."

"You know you'll burn a piece of toast… the only person I know can't boil an egg properly." She was laughing hard as fuck now causing me to laugh too cause she wasn't bullshitting. My high yella ass couldn't cook for shit. "Now take it… it's some fried ribs, collard greens, mac and cheese, yellow rice and a cornbread muffin."

My mouth was watering. Couldn't wait to go home and shower so I could tear my damn food up. "Whatever heffa… what's up with Cass… this was nice of him."

She shrugged. "He's legit… he's a businessman… and that's a plus. He's just helping me get back on my feet by letting me work here…" She rambled on. "We'll catch up later though."

"Aiight…" I hugged my friend and walked out. I was hoping to see the slick mouth ass lil girl at the register but she was gone so I walked out and sat in the car immediately getting pissed off that I didn't have any damn gas. I knew my car so I knew I could at least make it home, so I turned on my music loud and started heading home as I played Bad Bad Bad by Young Thug and Lil Baby… cause whenever I was in my car alone you couldn't tell me I wasn't a thug behind these tints. I rapped along speeding down 163rd street:

Rose gold seat on a fucking helicopter,
Double C, no Chanel, cause she bad, bad, bad,
Ridin' Kawasaki, and I could cop you a new Rari,
Let you ride it in your Rafs and you're bad, bad, bad,
No Playin, no Atari, I won't play with you for nothing,
I can eat you like Hibachi cause you bad, bad, bad,
I just took the doors off the Ghini now I'm riding,
And I'm still sliding in her sideways, now she call me her

zaddy.

I was almost to my house when I felt my shit coughing. “No no nooooo! Fuck! I knew I should’ve just gone to the damn gas station!” I hit my damn steering wheel easing off to the side of the road to avoid disrupting traffic with my hazards on in the middle of the street. I blew hard and let my head back on the headrest. Outside of work, this had been one long ass stressful day.

I pulled out my phone and called Latrell cause I knew he’d come. “Yo?” He answered.

“Nigga please… don’t pick up the phone like you talking to one of yo homeboy’s.” I said rolling my eyes.

He laughed. “You always talking shit… let me try this again. Good evening Abbey…how you doing?”

As bad as I tried to play shit cool with Trell it was getting harder and harder to ignore these butterflies that I felt so bad. Especially because I was betraying my friend. This was one of our number one rules… family was off limits, especially siblings cause if shit went sour it could complicate the entire well-being of our relationships. This is why eventually; I knew I had to stop fucking him. I smiled at the sound of his voice. “I need your help… I ran outta gas and I don’t have a gas can…”

He cut me off. “Even if you did have a can you ain’t got no business walking to no gas station by yo ’self anyway… where you at? Never mind just ping yo location and I’m comin’.” He told me before hanging up. I sat in the car and waited while scrolling my Instagram account. It took all of 30 minutes before he arrived but as soon as I saw his car pulling up behind me I hopped out. His music was loud as hell and from the front windshield, I could see he had somebody with him. A girl in the passenger seat.

Now see, I planned on being nice but now my attitude

was on a thousand about something I shouldn't even be giving a fuck about. I knew he fucked with other bitches; the shit was different actually seeing him with one of them. Trell hopped out wearing a pair of baggy Tru's, a black tee and some Timberland boots. His creed cologne was loud as hell as he walked up on me after removing the gas can from his trunk. "It's about time…" I rolled my eyes and removed the gas cap.

Trell ignored my attitude. "My bad man, I was in the middle of something when you called that's why it took so long but a nigga couldn't leave you out here stranded like that." As he poured I wanted to take my heel and kick him right in the ass, but I refrained from it. Lil pretty brown sat there staring at us both from the seat.

"Yeah, I appreciate that." I told him while trying to adjust my attitude. "Can you hurry up?"

He finished pouring and turned around after he closed the cap. "Man what's yo problem? You must've had a bad day…" He frowned at me and then licked his lips. "Either that or you want some of this dick."

"Oh please… go dick down one of them bitches cause I'm not hard up for it." I glanced at the car. I couldn't believe this nigga had the nerve to show up here with a bitch. I thought he had more respect for what we had going on but clearly he didn't. "Whose your little friend?" I asked him.

He tilt his head to the side giving me a little smirk. "Oh… so this where the attitude come from? I know tough ass Abbey ain't feelin' a way cause I got my friend with me. What was I supposed to do? Get rid of her and have you waiting out here or bring her along to come to yo rescue?"

I frowned. "Um don't flatter yo'self-fool…" I reached up and kissed his cheek. "Thanks for saving my ass…" I turned to walk away opening my car door prepared to get in.

He chuckled. “Yeah… aiight, you’ll be aiight.” He said cooley before he got in his car and pulled off before me. I sat for a few more minutes pissed with my damn self for almost showing my vulnerability. The nerve of him talking about ‘what was he supposed to do with her’… as far as I was concerned he should’ve put the bitch out on the corner of 79th street with the rest of them hoes.

Taking a deep breath, I finally took my ass home but I needed to stop by the farmers market and grab me something to drink first. One thing I couldn’t stand about being on the road was driving behind a muthafucka that acted like it was nowhere to go. “BONKK!” I sat on the horn trying to force the car in front of me to move the hell out of the way. “Movveee!”

The silver Mercedes slowed down and moved out the way just as we were coming up on a red light. Good cause I wanted to give the driver the evil ass look for driving so damn slow in a 45-mph speed zone doing at least 15. “Excuse me? Can I help you?” The green-eyed dude asked me with a funky ass look. He was so damn pretty I almost forgot what the fuck I wanted to say.

“Are you aware you’re doing 15 in a 45 miles per hour speed zone? Next time have some consideration for other people on the road!” I snapped.

Instead of him getting mad, he smiled. Oh Lord, his smile was everything. I tried so hard to be mad at him but he was so damn cute. “I don’t know who or what pissed you off but trust me bae… your day will get better.” He told me… that’s when I knew he was a little sweet. It wasn’t cause what he said, it was how he said it. “I’m driving so slow because my back tire is flat.”

“Damn,” I shook my head. “I’m sorry, I hadn’t even

noticed… look at me taking my frustrations out on you and you're in distress like I was a few minutes ago."

"It's okay… my man is laid back in this damn seat sleeping but I'm about to wake his ass up."

I tried to take a peek but dude really was leaned all the way back. It almost looked like the man was in the car alone. "Okay, well you okay? You need triple A or a jack? Anything I can do to help?"

"Umm yeah, I have a spare but I need a lug wrench. Do you have one sweetie?"

I frowned and thought about it. "I think I do… pull over out of the road and I'll give it to you. Might wanna go ahead and wake your man up cause ion know how to change a tire."

When I pulled over I followed right behind him and popped my trunk so he could get the wrench. I watched as he walked to the passenger seat and woke the dude up. From the front windshield of my car Leon and me locked eyes and my heart dropped. I didn't know whether to speak or to run so I just sat frozen with my heart racing. "What the fuck is going on?" I mumbled.

I could tell Leon was in an uncomfortable position; he was embarrassed. Neither did he want to speak to me. He simply changed the tire and got back in the car. "Thanks for everything love…" the guy extended his hand. "Don't mind my boyfriend, he's kinda shy… my name is Kevin."

I slowly shook his hand… and nod my head trying desperately to swallow the lump that had formed in my throat. "I..I…umm it's okay Kevin.. Glad I could help. You take care now."

I waited until they pulled off before I exhaled wondering why the fuck I had to be the one put in this position. "Damn Leon," I whispered still shaking my muthafucking head knowing damn well nobody knew what was up with him.

MAJESTIC JONES

"Where yo head at Leon?" I sat at the trap counting money while we waited for Trell to show up. In my opinion this nigga wasn't acting like his usual self but I didn't have time to babysit nobody's feelings. "What chick got you all caught up in yo feelings?" I asked.

He focused on bagging up the shit we needed and then adjusted his gun in the small of his waist. I knew Leon wasn't really a killer but growing up in the hood wasn't shit wrong with having some protection on you, cause these niggas would try to have one up on you at any given time.

"Nothin' bro… finals kickin' my ass.. that and I'm just focusin' on the paper." He said nonchalantly. This nigga had been doin' this weird ass shit lately all standoffish and not saying too much. Didn't bother me too much though cause ever since him and Trell started working for me shit was smooth, they were always on time, and never came up short. Which meant Poochie and me didn't have no problems. At times I felt like Poochie was just like my mama though. Nigga downed me for not being Malik.

Malik was one of his most loyal soldiers and he took his

death kinda hard but that ain't mean they had to give me a hard time. I'm a man though so I ate that shit up. If you wanted to survive in this game you couldn't show emotion cause that shit got niggas killed. That's one thing Malik taught me was to never show ya hand… so I didn't.

"Aight… aiight… cool… long as you good. Need you to be focused to make sure shit tight around here. It's the first of the month so you know today gone be a good day." I rubbed both my hands together and thinking about all the bread we were about to bring in. Shit, a nigga needed it too. My mama done called three times this week asking for money and cussed me out every time I didn't come. I had shit to do, but today I was gone make time. I walked away to answer the knocking coming from the back door of the trap. "Who is it?"

"You know who it is…. open the door."

"Who?"

"Nigga open the fuckin' door… come on."

I opened it and let Trell in as he shot past me with his gun in one hand while he held a duffle bag in the other. He dropped the bag on the table and clapped his brother up. "All the money there…" he pointed. "I had to fuck one of your lil corner boys up tryna hustle me but everything a hunnid with the bread."

That was the difference between Leon and Latrell. Leon was the quieter one. The most strategic, while Latrell had more of a hot head. If he had in his mind he was gone shoot somebody… that nigga would do it with no hesitation, which is why it was a super plus to have them working for me cause I could keep my eyes on these niggas for when it was time to execute my plan. Seeing them two together being able to have brotherly bonding moments and shit killed my fucking soul. It amazed me how everybody just forgot what LeLe did to my brother. They got their sister back from the system, plus they had each other too, but mine wasn't coming back from the grave and muthafuckas would have to eventually pay for that. I wanted everybody to feel my fucking pain. "Cool… cool…" I sat down and counted the money again myself for reassurance.

After another few hours I left them there knowing they'd handle business cause they were just like that. Loyalty at its best… that and they needed that paper to keep up with the college life. I knew if their parent's or LeLe knew what they were up to they'd have a fucking fit but they couldn't blame me. These were two grown ass niggas and ain't no way I could just ruin their lives for them; the shit was their choice. They could've said no but they didn't cause they trust me.

I called Poochie to see where he wanted to meet up. "Yo… you at the drop spot?"

"Nah… had to come handle some business at Jazzy's… just drop the bread off here and I'll take it from there."

"Cool… see you in a few." I hung up. Now this shit was outta the norm cause he never handled this kinda business at the lounge. He always kept his street life and his business life separate from each other. When I pulled up he was standing next to Trey outside of his Bentley since that's what he was riding in today. These niggas killed me… it's seven days in a week and outta seven days they had on suits at least four. Some badass suits too. Guess this the shit that came with being a Boss.

I hopped out and popped my trunk to grab the bag. Trey walked up to me taking them from me. "Wus good fool…" he spoke and walked off to the inside. That nigga was like that though. He wasn't too big on being friendly with niggas. Matter fact only nigga I ever really seen him talk to was Poochie. Trey was just a straight up thug and trigger-happy. He'd kill niggas for breakfast if that's what he needed to do so most of the time niggas just stayed out of his way. You'd never see him with any bitch he was fucking. Nobody knew who his family was, how much money he really had or none of that. Poochie on the other hand… nigga spend that money like it was nothing and loved being flashy. He'd murk a nigga quick but he wasn't silent about his success and he was using his Lounge to wash up all his drug money to make himself seem like he was legit.

"That nigga don't never say shit…" I shook my head and clapped Poochie up. He was smoking a cigar and just staring at me before he spoke.

"He's a smart nigga… one of the smartest I know. You can learn some shit from him." He told me without cracking so much as a smile. "What's the deal with shorty?" He asked.

I frowned. "Who?"

"LeLe… the chick you put me on nigga… the one who killed Malik…. Shorty don't seem like she's this evil hearted ass broad. Don't get me wrong I don't want the nigga death to go in vain… and she still ain't told me the story yet, but I'm a pretty good judge of character. Shorty ain't evil… she's remorseful as fuck."

Nigga was about to piss me off. The fuck was he even talking about right now. "I told you drag the bitch not fall in love with her muthafuckin' ass cause that's what it seems like."

"First of all you better remember who the fuck you talking to for one. For two I'll handle my muthafuckin' business however I choose. I ask you one simple question. You can miss me with all the other shit. This ain't got shit to do with being in love. I barely know the muthafuckin' girl." He growled.

I stood down. I couldn't let my anger and assumptions have me beefing with this nigga. "You right.. my bad fool.

Just let them emotions get the best of me. I mean… she aiight I guess but the bitch can't be too remorseful. She has yet to apologize to me or my mama so you can take that for what it is."

He leaned back against his car taking in what I had said to him. The front door of Jazzy's swung open and LeLe was walking with her head down removing something from the pocket of her apron. "Hey Cass… I'm done with the special for today all they gotta do is…" She stop talking when she looked up locking eyes with me. I could tell she wanted to turn around and go the other way. "OH my fault I didn't know you were busy… hi Majestic." She spoke from where she stood.

Poochie motioned for her to come over to us where she slowly walked over. "What's good shorty… long time ma." I nod my head. "You rushed outta your welcome home party so fast a nigga ain't get to speak to you. I would've stop by ya crib but a nigga been real busy." It took everything in me not to slap the taste outta her mouth.

Her eyes adverted from Poochie to me and she gave me a slight smile. "Yeah… I had to go… how's your mother been? I wanted to stop by and see her but it's been crazy trying to get back on my feet."

"Is that right?" I stroked my goatee just staring at her. Bitch was still beautiful.

"Aiight man… I gotta get this business situated so I'll holla at you…." Poochie excused me. I didn't understand why the nigga was coming to her rescue sensing that she was uncomfortable but shit had me tight.

I nod my head and reached in to give her a hug. She tensed up but hugged me back. "Be easy sis… see you around and welcome home shorty."

"Thank you…" She said in almost a whisper.

I walked off and hopped in my car watching them two engulfed in a conversation. I really hoped this nigga Poochie ain't plan on being with her forreal on no knight and shining armor type shit. He had one job, get her ass comfortable and make her life hell like torture… bitch ain't deserve to come home and live a happy life, not as long as I was breathing.

A short time after I pulled up to my mama's house ignoring all the lil badass kids running around outside. "Ma!"

She sat on the couch with a whole bottle of vodka in her hand. "Where's my money?"

I immediately got pissed off. I couldn't babysit the streets and babysit her ass too. "You turning into a fucking drunk… this all you do is drink!" I snatched the bottle from her hand and poured the shit down the kitchen drain. I wasn't even aware she had gotten up from the couch until I felt her attacking me from behind.

I tried to duck the blows she had coming to the back of my head. "Chill the fuck out!" I growled grabbing her arms trying to ignore the burning from the scratches she had all over my neck.

"You little motherfucker you! Don't you come in here trying to tell me what the fuck to do! I'm grown! You can't tell me how to grieve!"

"And don't you throw your life away like this! You think this would make him happy?? He's probably rolling around in his fucking grave!"

"Until you've lost a child don't you tell me shit you don't nothing about! This pain never goes away! Never!" She cried falling over in my arms.

I felt bad for my mama… only thing I could do was press her nappy head into my chest and allow her to get it all out. Wasn't shit I could say to make her happy and obviously nothing I tried to do helped. In my honest opinion she needed to go back to work or else she really was gone turn into a fucking drunk. She already had one foot in the door and one foot out. I walked her back to the couch and sat her down. "Ma I got the money for you. I got some extra too okay? I want you to get your hair done. Then I want you to go get a nice pedicure and massage. I'll take you out to dinner this week. I need you to get outta this house."

She sniffed and wiped her tears. Instead of arguing with me she slowly nod her head and stood up to go grab yet another fucking bottle from the cabinet. I just shook my head. "That'll be nice… I do need to get out of this house…" she poured a shot and took it to the head. "You need to have me some grandbabies or something. Maybe if I had some grand-kids it'll give me something to do. You need a nice young lady. When are you gone bring somebody home for me to meet?"

I'd been so caught up in making my money that love was the furthest thing from my mind. I didn't even have time to commit to nobody for that matter. That shit just simply wasn't in the plan right now. I had way too much shit going on to give somebody the type of time they would require that's why I fucked with bitches who didn't care about that. As long as we were on the same page we were good. "Soon ma… soon." I lied grabbing my keys. I kissed her on the cheek after giving her the money I promised along with some more and headed out. I was in dying need to get my dick sucked, or some pussy one… but it needed to be from somebody who was down with the same shit.

KIMBERLEY "KIM" LAWS

The party that I was finishing the touches on had to been one of my best pieces of work for a kid's party. The little boy 'Troy' was turning three- and the-party theme was Toy Story. I had made some good money from doing this party so it was only right that I pulled out all of my best tricks. I displayed a candy table with all the goodies and I had balloon arches all over the place. I had draped the party tent with a bunch of different colors and made sure the table linen and chair covers were perfect too. It had taken me all of about 6 hours to do everything and sometimes I really wished I had a team. Having a team meant splitting money and I wasn't down with splitting my money with nobody. This was some money I sure didn't wanna split and I'm sure they had plenty of it with all the shit they had at this party. Looked like a mini carnival with all the rides. I was convinced that they had to be some dope dealers. Everybody who'd come in and out dropping shit off looked like thugs with money.

"Hey Kim… this is beautiful girl. I appreciate you so much. Poochie said you were good. I didn't know it was this damn good though." My client CoCo squealed pleased with my work. I used the back of my hand to wipe the sweat from my forehead and took a seat.

"Poochie?" I quizzed. I don't know no Poochie. "Tell him I said, 'thanks for the referral though' I appreciate that."

"Oh I'm sorry girl. Calling the nigga by his street name. You probably know him as Cass." She corrected herself. "His friend Trey is my brother."

I sure didn't know him as no damn Poochie. That was very interesting though. Wonder why he acted like two different people. I could bet that nigga had a whole other life. The suits and shit was just a front. "Oh right… okay yes I know him." I smiled thinking about his fine ass.

"Un Un girl I know that look on females." She shook her head laughing. "You don't even wanna fuck with him trust me… it ain't even worth the problems that nigga bring. Looks nice but all this shit comes with a price." I really examined CoCo again. She had on hella ice. I didn't know if she had gotten her body done or not but that shit was banging. Her CoCo colored skin glistened and her long silky weave flowed down her back.

"I'll keep that in mind. I'm so glad you like it cause this really put me to work. I'm feeling how I feel whenever I get done training somebody." I laughed.

"Damn…" She giggled admiring my work. "And you still have to do the that candy table for the inside too… don't forget." She reminded me.

I hopped up. "Shit… I forgot about that. Let me get to it now." I looked at my watch. It was 2:15pm. "What time are you expecting guest?"

"Girl the party starts at 3 but you know how that is… black people time it'll be about 4."

"Okay I can do it… shouldn't take me that long. Let me run to the restroom real quick and I'll get to it."

I rushed inside and ran into the stall to pee. When I was done I wiped and pulled my spandex back up before placing some tissue on the seat to sit on it. Although I had on my tights I didn't want to be touching the nasty ass toilet. The Michael Kor fanny pack I had around my waist was perfect to hold all of my little belongings in it so I rummaged through it until I found what I was looking for. I rushed and opened the tiny bag of coke and then dipped my pinky nail in it bringing it up to my nostril where I sniffed. I instantly held my head back and pinch the bridge of my nose. When I was satisfied I did the same thing only this time I rubbed it on my teeth and in my mouth.

I gave it a few minutes to get that feeling I was looking for. I needed the adrenaline if I was gonna get through this cause a bitch was tired as hell. I made sure my nose was clean before walking out and then I went to grab everything I needed to do the extra candy table. I'd been so busy doing my party planning that I hadn't had time to really fuck with anybody or fuck with anybody for that matter. I had my eyes on that nigga Cass but he curved me like a motherfucker at LeLe's welcome home party so I was stuck with what I knew. Crazy that he called just as I thought about his ass. "Where you at?" Majestic asked as soon as I answered.

I was trying to hold the damn phone and grab the big ass box I needed for the table. "What you want? I was just thinking about you." I told him truthfully as I licked my lips.

"You know what I want…"

"Umm hmmm… I'll call you as soon as I leave from doing this party."

"Damn you always on the go… I respect it tho… gotta get that money."

This nigga was a trip but he did have some good dick so

whatever. “Yeah, cause I can’t wait for a nigga to take care of me… you damn sho ain’t.”

“You not even my bitch so why would I do that?”

I rolled my eyes. This nigga was blowing my high. “Yeah, yeah, yeah… anyway I’ll call you I gotta go.” I hung up.

It took me damn near an hour to finish the job completely but I was in love. After taking all of my pictures to upload to my Instagram account I left the party. It took me a few minutes to put some of the boxes back in the U-Haul truck that I’d rented to transport everything but I eventually got it together. I drove with the AC blasting and made my way through the hot ass Miami streets. I couldn’t wait to get home and kick my damn feet up after showering. Since I didn’t have to be back out to pick up all of my shit from the party until later in the evening, that’s just what I planned to do.

I fussed when I got home realizing that someone had taken over my personal parking spot so I had to park in the apartment building on the side of mine in a visitor spot. I wish I knew who it was cause their ass would’ve been as good as cussed the fuck out. I found a black permanent marker and a piece of paper and left it on their windshield warning them that next time I’m calling the fucking tow.

Much to my surprise, Abbey was on my porch waiting for me dressed down in her skinny jeans, white Nikes and a tank top. Her hair was pulled back in a sleek ponytail and her freckles were popping on her fresh skin giving her a youthful look. “What you doing here and why you look all mad?” I fumbled for my keys before unlocking the door. Abbey followed me inside and closed the door.

“First of all I didn’t know I needed permission to come check on yo ass, and second I’m not mad… a bitch is hot as fuck. That sun ain’t no joke.”

“Yeah, it’s hot as fuck… anyway what’s up?”

"Un un don't what's up me Kim, there's something I need to do before I get to talking."

I wasn't paying her ass no mind at first but I quickly spun around wondering what she needed to do. "What?"

Before I could even get the words out good her entire hand was coming across my left cheek as she slapped the fuck out of me. SLAP!

I grabbed my face… what the fuck? I was all prepared to haul off and slap her ass back as soon as I regrouped. "Next time you collect some money that belongs to me and don't tell me. I'mma fuck yo ass up Kimberly. I know you spent my damn money cause if you hadn't you would've called me. I'mma let this one slide but don't ever play me like that again." She walked away and grabbed a cold bottle of water from my fridge taking a sip before she sat down on the couch.

I was still holding my fucking face in shock from the stinging but she was right. I had to let her have this one. I did collect her money and I didn't tell her. I unintentionally spent her shit too. I had been holding on to it but some unexpected shit came up and I used it not thinking she would mind… still I should've told her. For that, I did look flaw. "Aiight." I rubbed my face tasting the blood in my mouth. "You know what… you right I should've told you. That's my fault for taking your shit. I'll pay you back."

"I don't even want the money. It's the principal." She explained. "You know we only put up with your shit cause you like a sister but you got some stupid ass ways."

"Yeah well… I always been the black sheep it's nothing new. My step daddy was a fucking child molester and my mama only really gave a fuck about Karter. She never wanted to have two kids in the first place. She always loved 'Baby A' and it was fuck 'Baby B'." I rolled my eyes shaking bad memories from my mind. Shit I didn't wanna think about. I didn't expect nobody to understand me cause at times I didn't even understand myself. A lot shit I've done I still ain't forgave myself… it's a lot of more shit I might do and probably won't forgive that either. Hell, what can I say? I'm damaged goods and a work in progress.

Abbey softened up a bit when she saw a tear drop from my eye. I quickly wiped it away. "Damn, you wanna talk about it Kim? We can talk between us."

I plopped down on the couch. "Nah… I know you didn't just come over here to slap the shit out of me so what else brings you here?"

I watched Abbey look nervous all of a sudden. "Umm, I need some advice about some shit I came across and I don't know if I should tell it or mind my fucking business."

"Okayyy… ummm who does it concern?"

"See, that's the thing… it concerns one person but it involves everybody. You know the way society set up people can be opinionated as fuck."

I agreed. "Well you know what I think? I think you should just mind your own business. This world would be a much better place if muthafuckas did just that." I told her opening my fanny pack to grab my small bag of weed to roll us a joint. In the process my little bag of coke fell out. "Shit…" I reached over and went to pick it up.

Abbey was quicker. "Kim, what the fuck is this?" She asked with her face all balled up dangling the little bag. "I know damn well this ain't what I think it is." I tried to grab it from her but she quickly snatched back.

"You know how a few seconds ago I gave you that advice about people minding their own business? Yeah well, this is one of those times. I'm good trust me."

"What the fuck do you mean you good? When did you even start snorting this shit? Nah Kim this ain't it."

"About two years ago." I admitted to her. "And I got it under control. People have their own ways of dealing with shit and this is mine now give me my shit Abbey." I felt myself getting agitated for being so damn careless.

She looked disgusted but gave it back to me. "You know what? On that note, I'mma go. I'll call you later girl I just can't even deal with this shit right now." Abbey grabbed her keys and left me alone. As soon as she opened the door she screamed and grabbed her chest.

"Ahhh! Damn Majestic you scared the fuck outta me! What are you even doing here?"

"Yeah," I chimed in. "I told you I was gone call you."

He stepped inside. "You took too long and I knew yo ass was here." He chuckled. He then gave Abbey a kiss on the cheek. "What up ma…"

"Hey…" She looked at us both figuring some shit was up. "It's only one reason why he could be here and for that ya'll so nasty. I'm gone… and don't forget to strap up!" She yelled behind her.

"Damn Majestic... what I tell you bout popping up over here?"

Majestic didn't say shit, he looked at me with lust in his eyes. I couldn't even be mad at him either. We had a mutual understanding. He wasn't shit and neither was I. In reality we were both damaged goods dealing with different circumstances of pain in our lives. He didn't have time to love anybody and I didn't either, so what we were doing now was working for us both. He had his hoes and I had my niggas. I didn't tell him what to do and he didn't tell me what to do. "Com'ere…"

I shook my head while smiling at his fine ass. "Nah… I need to shower. You can join me if you want to." I slowly walked away removing my tight clothes from my body piece by piece. Majestic's eyes followed my naked body all the way to the bathroom. I turned on the hot water and shook my hand underneath it until I felt it warming up and to make sure it was the right temperature. "You coming?!" I yelled when I got in. The warm water felt good cascading down my body urging me to close my eyes and take it all in.

When I opened them back up, it was only because I felt the presence of Majestic watching me. A few seconds ago I was all down for him watching me walk away, but now I felt some kind of way. I didn't like it… the way he was looking at me gave me the creeps. It wasn't because it was him. It was because my stepdaddy did the same shit to me when I was younger… right before he touched me and did whatever he wanted with my body. "I'll be right out." I slid the shower door completely closed so he could no longer stare at me.

I didn't have to see his face to know that he was beyond confused. "What? You just wanted me to come in here with you now you want me to get out? See, this why I don't want a relationship with nobody cause women are confusing as fuck."

I didn't even know I tuned him out until I realized I hadn't heard not one word that he'd said. Whatever he said didn't even matter because all the fucked-up thoughts I tried so hard to keep out of my head were now swarming around me like fish and I hated it. Nobody knew the darkness that I encountered on a daily and nobody gave enough of fuck to even ask. If Majestic was a different type of nigga I would've spoke to him about my problems but he wasn't. If I knew that he even cared about me just a little bit then maybe I would actually open up. I couldn't say I didn't care about him though cause as a person, truth is, I did. However, I knew he was one person I could never get what I wanted and that was to be loved… and I knew this cause we were just alike.

When I stepped out of the shower Majestic sat waiting for me on the toilet with his hand propped up under his chin. The smoke from the hot water surrounded the bathroom and fogged up the mirror behind him so I couldn't even see myself to make sure my facial expression wasn't showing what I felt. "I'll get you right in a few minutes… I just need a minute."

I could tell he wanted to say something but instead he walked out of the bathroom giving me some privacy. I made sure he was gone before I locked the door and pulled my makeup bag from under the sink. I pulled out a small bag of coke and dipped my white tipped fingernail in there before bringing it back up to my nose where I sniffed in both nostrils this time and threw my head back holding the bridge of my nose. Emotionally this shit always made me feel better. As long as I had it under control, I didn't see the problem. Even if I did… I just couldn't stop.

A few minutes later I walked out with my towel around me to go find Majestic. Sitting in my room on my Queen size bed he was holding the remote to my fire stick flipping through channels. His deep brown eyes stared at me when he notice me walk in. "What the fuck goin' on with you Kim? I'm not feelin' this shit no more ma… this ain't even you and ion wanna be here just givin' you no dick if we aint on the same page. I know I'm an asshole and all but it's some shit I actually do give a fuck about."

I was cool with him not wanting to fuck no more cause neither did I. Instead I walked over to my vanity and lotion down my body. "If you're referring to giving a fuck about me then don't… do us both a favor and just don't."

"I wasn't referring to actually giving a fuck about in that kinda way you crazy ass girl. What I'm saying is it ain't like I aint known you half my life so yeah… if something bothering you I may wanna know and it has nothing to do with us fucking."

"Yeah well… I'm aiight."

"No you ain't but if you don't wanna tell me I won't beg. You got some shit with you Kim… a lot of shit. I think that's why you act out the way you do."

I didn't like where this conversation was going, more so cause he was making me feel vulnerable and at the end of the day I didn't owe nobody shit. "Oh yeah Majestic? And why do you act the way you do huh? Spill your beans… own your shit. You're trying to compete with a dead man Majestic…. You're out here being somebody you're not trying to earn respect that you already have. You have it cause of whose little brother you are but you have yet to accept it cause you want to be respected for you." I pointed to my chest. "This is me you're talking to… not some random hoe… this is Kim… I know what the fuck is going on."

I could tell what I said had gotten to him by the discomfort on his face. He sucked his teeth. "You don't know shit Kim… that's not even half of it but while you on my shit let's get on yours. You hate yourself that's why you don't respect yourself yo… that's why you feel insecure or jealous about every bitch around you… even the ones that love you. Truth be told you despise your own fucking sister… your twin, the same one you shared a womb with and why is that Kim? What you thought I ain't know? I'm very observant."

I felt like I'd been hit in the damn stomach. "You don't know shit so watch your mouth. You don't know what it's like being the one that was regretted. They loved Karter, did everything for Karter and from the age of 14… I had to work for everything I got while they gave her everything for free! She didn't even try to speak up for me she just sucked it all in! And you wanna know something? SHE STILL HAS IT

ALL! HAPPY LIFE! FIANCE! BABY ON THE WAY! AND especially the love from our mother." I didn't even realize I was shaking or crying until I felt the warm water from my eyes hit my bare thigh.

"Damn…" He sighed walking over to me and started rubbing my back. "Sometimes you gotta let that shit out. It's okay to cry."

"Well then why don't you take your own advice sometimes then?" I sniffed and wiped my eyes. I hated looking weak as fuck. "You're angry! A blind man can see that! You're living in a fucked up dark place and if you don't do something about it you'll end up doing something you may regret!" Majestic didn't say anything at all… "You've got some hidden agendas dude… you got secrets too…" I lowered my voice in almost a whisper. "We all have secrets."

Majestic sat next to me as we both let our minds saunter away in our own thoughts. I remembered I used to have dreams about a Knight in shining armor and happy endings. That just didn't exist in my world. It would take a special kind of person to save my heart. With the way my life was going I had way too many demons and I just couldn't see that happening. I looked in Majestic's eyes again and saw a hurt little boy.

It was a lot I wanted to tell him… there were things I wanted to share with him. I wished I could tell him about my snorting habit. I wished I could tell him what led to that. I just simply wished I had the courage to tell him about Malik and me… my first true love. When he chose LeLe over me I was devastated… but when he died… I was crushed. A part of me left that day. My best friend became the little white bag that took all my pain away… and I had to hide this shit from everybody… even Majestic, the same nigga I often felt myself falling for and had to dig those thoughts right back out. If Majestic just acted like himself it's easy to fall for him. I felt like I was wrong for betraying Malik but Malik betrayed me first. He never cared about me he fucked me and sent me on my way knowing how I felt about him. I couldn't even tell anyone about us… not even my friends… then he met LeLe and fell in love.

Thinking of LeLe put a salty taste in my mouth. She was always in my way. I had a weird type of love hate relationship with her… like I'd beat a bitch ass for her but at the same time I despised her… everybody wanted LeLe. I could barely get anybody to give a shit about me. Snapping out of my thoughts. I walked over to my drawer and slipped a silk gown over my head and on my body. "I'mma lay down Majestic… you can let yourself out."

He took the Timbs he was wearing off. "I'mma chill for a lil bit… go to sleep."

This is the first time he ever said some shit like that. Nobody had ever stayed at my place. They got what they wanted and went on about their business. Since he wasn't a stranger in my life I allowed it. I didn't even realize I fell asleep until I woke up in the middle of the night. Majestic was long gone but he made sure to lock my bottom lock. "Fuck it…" I mumbled shooting CoCo a text letting her know I'd pick up all my stuff in the morning. I set the alarm and cuddled back under my covers praying that nightmares didn't fuck with me tonight.

LEANDRA 'LELE' WELLS

"Cass this shit is heavy…" I used the back of my hand to wipe the sweat from my forehead before placing my hands on the lower part of my back just looking around at all the shit he had in his garage. I had been busting my ass for weeks and I was so thankful for Cass giving me that job. I truly did enjoy cooking and spent a lot of my days going through different cookbooks to add different things to the menu. This is the first day Cass ever brought me to his house since I told him the kitchen at Jazzy's needed a makeover. It needed to feel more like home to the cooks instead of just a job. When he informed me he had a bunch of shit in his garage that we could use for the kitchen; I was ecstatic but now I was tired as hell from trying to lift and move all of this stuff.

Cass sat down going through some paperwork wearing a bare ripped chest and a pair of Tru Religion jeans. A cigar hung from his mouth. "Nobody told you to come over here and try to be superwoman either. I only told you to come look at the shit so we could see what you wanted. Shit, I ain't tell you come over here on yo incredible hulk shit."

I wanted to curse his slick mouth ass out but I laughed instead cause he was right. I did kinda jump the gun. "Whatever…" I told him flopping down in the chair. He'd already taken me on a tour of this big ass empty house and when I say empty; I meant empty as in nobody to share it with. "Cass, this house has 5 bedrooms, 3 bathrooms, a living room, a sitting room, a dining room, an office, and a man's cave. Can you please tell me why you need all of this?"

Cass finally looked up from the paperwork he was looking through and briefly stared at me. He shrugged. "Haven't found the right woman to share it with but when I do, it'll be hers too. If she pisses me off I'll just go to my other house… won't be no breaking up. We'll have all the space we need."

"You mean to tell me you have another house?"

"Yep, just as big as this one… matter fact we can be in that house together for days and not have to see each other if we don't want to. That's how big that shit is."

"Wow." I mumbled. "Must be nice…"

"It is…." He replied nonchalantly.

"So who lives there?"

"Nobody… just me when I feel like it. Got a nanny that comes through too but she don't stay long. She clean up, do her thing and gone about her business."

I knew I wasn't the smartest bitch in the world but I just couldn't see how he was able to have all of this money off of Jazzy's. "Cass, listen… you're cool and all and I really do appreciate you but if you're into some illegal shit I need to know. Like you have all this money, which is cool but I used to be the fiancé of a dope boy so I know how this shit goes. I can almost smell the dirty money before I can even see it. I just need to know because you know my situation."

He pulled a seat in front of me forcing us to be eye to eye.

"I mean ma, I know your situation… but I really don't cause you still haven't told me. What ever happen to your fiancé? I mean, I know you were locked up for manslaughter but I need to know the rest."

My eyes got so big. "I never told you that so who the fuck told you my business?" I fumed feeling my eyes water up. I didn't know why I got so mad so quickly but I did. I didn't want my situation brought up or for anybody to be talking about it. "It was Majestic's bitch ass wasn't it?"

Cass frowned. "Yo, calm down LeLe. Majestic aint tell me shit. The shit is public records so I searched it up my damn self… online. You couldn't have thought I was just gon' let you work for me without knowing shit about you. What if you were a sex offender, or..or.. a scam artist or some shit? I got you at my place of business around my peoples; I would need to know some shit like that."

"I'm not none of those things!" I shook my head and crossed my arms over my chest. "I can't believe you did that! You could've just asked me!"

"The fuck? I tried! You don't talk… you don't say shit… all you do is cook and go the fuck home."

"Wrong… I cook, stack my money, and go the fuck home." I sniffed and wiped my eyes. "Please don't ever do that to me again. My shit is sensitive Cass; you could never understand."

He grabbed both my hands into his and looked me in the eyes. "Okay I won't, but I need you to tell me what's the deal. I'm not a dope boy if that's what you thinking. I'm a corporate thug… but I'm legit. I know how you feel being around certain shit but that ain't the case with me."

I snatched my hands away from him. I don't know why certain things I did, I felt like Malik were still here and I needed to respect him. I took a long deep breath and exhaled.

"I…it was a mistake Cass." I started tearing up again. "I had just turned 22 years old. Malik had proposed to me and we went out to enjoy my birthday. We both were fucked up and I made him let me drive. I put my seat belt on but not his…" I took a minute to reflect on the last moments of his life. Malik looked so peaceful sleeping in the passenger seat that night. "I think I dozed off because I ended up running us off of the road and he was ejected from the car… he died on the scene Cass…" I cried like it had just happened. "He died on the scene and I couldn't save him. He lost his life because of me and I lost a part of me… that's why I went to jail. I'm a murderer."

Cass stood up and consoled me allowing me to drop all of my tears on his chest. "Nah you ain't no murderer ma. It could've happened another way if that's what was meant to happen. It wasn't your fault LeLe and you can't blame yourself for the rest of yo life or you'll kill yourself."

I heard what he was saying but it felt like a relief getting it off of my chest. I rarely spoke about my situation, even in jail I just always avoided it. "Yeah, I guess you're right." I sighed and wiped my face. "I'm sorry for all these damn tears… I know I look so weak."

"Nah you good man… you aiight. You needed to let it out."

We both averted our attention to the garage door entrance where Trey was standing staring at us. I wasn't even aware that he was here. "Everything aiight?" He asked cooley. Every time I saw Trey he was so damn serious. He barely spoke at all and I could tell he didn't really trust people but one thing he did do was always ask me if I was okay. He was so damn fine too; matter of fact… he got finer every time I saw him especially with that chocolate skin. His entire body was covered in tats from the neck down.

"Yeah… it's cool." Cass told him.

Trey nod his head and then directed his question to only me. "LeLe you aiight?"

"Yeah I'm okay… just having a moment."

He reverted his attention back to Cass. "I got everything… I'mma head out. I should be back in town by tomorrow night."

"Good… good." Cass told him. "I'll make sure I drop CoCo that bread too."

"Aiight…"

Cass answered a call on his phone and stepped away a couple of feet. The call was quick but I didn't hear shit he was saying. When he hung up, he rushed to flag Trey down who was already backing out the driveway in his black Range Rover with the red guts on the inside. "Yo! I need you to drop LeLe off for me. Something came up!" He didn't have to tell me twice. I just got my belongings and said my goodbye. I wanted to head home anyway. "Hol' up." He told me before he ran inside the house. He came back out a few seconds later. "Here's a stack for the week."

I eyeballed the money. "You already paid me my thousand for this week."

"It's a bonus… you deserve it now take the money. Go buy something nice… do something with ya hair… shit something… ion know. You ain't did nothing to ya shit in weeks." He frowned using his hand to try to brush up the tresses falling from my sloppy bun. "I wanna finish this conversation later though." He told me looking deep into my eyes. I felt those familiar butterflies along with the throbbing in between my legs. I tried so hard not to like Cass in that kind of way but it was becoming so hard to ignore the feeling he gave me. Being around him every day seemed to mend my heart a little piece by piece. Sometimes I truly did feel like outside of me working for him… maybe, just maybe… he was really trying to save my heart.

I playfully slapped his hand away and took the money. "Whatever." I walked away and hopped in the truck with Trey. He didn't say anything to me when I got in, he just turned the music up and drove with one hand bobbing his head to the music. I was surprised that he wasn't even playing no rap shit. Instead, he played Computer Love:

Computer love (computer, computer love)
Computer love (lookin' for my computer love)
Computer love (hey)
Computer love (computer love)
You know I've been searching for someone
Who can share that special love with me
And your eyes have that glow
Could it be your face I see on my computer screen?
Need a special girl (ooh yeah)
To share in my computer world
I no longer need astrology
Thanks to modern technology
Shooby doo bop shoo doo bop I want to love you
Shooby doo bop (I want to love you) computer love
Shooby doo bop shoo doo bop I want to love you
Shooby doo bop my computer love

I wanted to laugh so badly cause he was so focused. His thick brows were slightly furrowed and his long lashes could be seen from the side. The hand he was steering the wheel with was covered with a scorpion tattoo and he wasn't paying me any attention. Since he had his panoramic sunroof back the humid Miami weather had my hair flying. This was the second time I had to catch a ride with Trey so he already knew where I lived. The less he spoke about himself the more I wanted to know. Like why the hell was he so mysterious?

I reached up to turn the music down. He gently slapped my hand away and did it for me. "Don't you know not to touch a man's radio? What's wrong ma?" He asked still focusing on the road.

I frowned. "Why don't you ever talk Trey? I mean, we all have shit with us but why you so uptight? You too fine to be so uptight."

"And you too smart to be so gullible…" He shrugged.

"What the fuck does that mean?"

He shook his head. "Nothing."

I knew he was lying but I didn't wanna push the issue. "What you mean Trey?"

"Leave it alone…" He replied. "So what up? What you plan on doing with yaself?"

"I'm doing what I need to do to survive. I'm a cook, that's what I do, what do you mean? Shit, what you plan on doing with yourself? Be Cass's do boy forever?"

Trey chuckled. "Watch ya mouth kidd… I'm not nobody's do boy. I'm my own man. I handle mine and I handle it well. I got my own plans. Sometimes you gotta use certain shit as a stepping stool but that don't mean you get content with that."

I thought about what he'd just said… he was absolutely right but did he feel like I was settling? "So you feel like I'm settling?"

"It's not my job to feel anything when it comes to you. That's something you gotta ask yourself and take it from there. All I'm saying is don't be no fool…. Take ya ass back to school and get that degree you were tryna get before you went in." He turned the music back up not even giving me a chance to respond. I didn't even know how he knew about me but I was no longer asking nobody shit or tryna figure out shit. This is my life and my testimony and I'll deal with it.

When Trey let me out in front of my house, I stood in the

driveway watching until he hit the corner. I then slowly drag my feet inside of the house still replaying our conversation. From the looks of it everybody was home. Trell let me in smacking on a bag of Doritos and a frozen cup. "Ouuu my favorite why you aint get me one?" I snatched his out his hand and begin to lick on it. "You don't even know if I ate some pussy today and you licking all over my shit… how it taste?" He mushed jokingly mushed me in the head.

"You so fucking nasty?" I gave him back his frozen cup. I didn't give a shit what he did with it after that. I looked my brother up and down. "You been looking like a whole lotta money lately… you and Leon both and I been meaning to talk to ya'll about that. What the hell ya'll got going on? Cause I know college money aint paying for all this shit and neither one of ya'll got a job so don't try to lie to me.

"Look, don't come in here acting like mama… I'm my own man aiight? As long as I'm doing what I gotta do."

"Um hmmm… you just better not let me find out. I don't care how big you are… I'll still fuck ya'll up."

Leon walked from the back room with his keys in his hand. "Fuck who up? I'll toss ya lil ass LeLe." He kissed me on the cheek. They think they had it all figured out but they wasn't gone be satisfied until they ass ended up right where I'd just come from.

"Tssss." I hissed under my breath. "I just hope ya'll aint dumb enough to be…"

"Dumb enough for what? What ya'll kids in here talking about now?" George coughed walking from the foyer scaring the shit out of us. George had really aged over the years. Still looked good but had a whole lot of grey hair now. I personally felt like at 55 years old he needed to retire his construction job cause it was taking a toll on his body.

"Don't you even worry about it old man…" Leon pat

George on the back and draped one arm around his neck. “Just talking about how we gone get rich and make sure you and ma don’t ever gotta work again.”

“Yeah…” Trell nod his head. “Allat.”

“Chile please…” I sassed.

“How you holding up LeLe? How’s the job?” George quizzed.

“It’s real good… I’m making real good money but I’m going to enroll back in school soon.” I shrugged. “I’ve been saving up my money so I can get a place and everything.”

“You don’t have to rush… me and your mother aren’t trying to push you out there.” He assured me.

I smiled. “I know…”

“Alright well I’m about to head on out so ya’ll make sure to lock up if you leave. Your mama went to play bingo.” He said with his lips balled up. “She don’t ever win shit, aint won in years and just keeps on going down there. I can’t figure this shit out for the life of me.” He grabbed his coat coughing again. A terrible cough.

“Yo, you aiight George?” Trell pat his back. He nod his head.

“I’m okay…. Just getting old. Ya’ll kids lock up.” He said again before heading out.

Leon was staring at me after locking the door. “What??” I asked.

“Ain’t no what… so you been running round with that nigga Cass a lot lately huh?”

“It ain’t even like that… he’s just my Boss and he’s helping me, that’s all.”

“Yeah well, what you giving him cause ain’t no nigga helping you for free.” Trell chimed in.

“I’m not no weak ass bitch… I got this…” I rolled my eyes at them both.

"Yeah… aiight." They both replied in unison.

"Well I'm out… I'mma holla at ya'll." Leon told us before he left. "Yo Trell…. Tonight. Same spot." He said.

Trell slapped hands with him and gave him a brotherly hug. "Aiight cool, I'mma be there after I make one stop. Gotta drop of this money to Bam." He sighed like he had a problem with it.

"And… what's the issue?" Leon asked.

"Just tired of dealing with his gay ass assistant. Fuck nigga sweeter than the sugar in Kool-aide and I hate the way he fucking looks at me. Nigga be wanting to break his fucking neck. You know how I feel bout that Queer ass shit man. To each its own; I'm not discriminating but I'll fucking kill the nigga he ever try me on that dumb ass shit."

Leon didn't reply… instead he just nod his head agreeing and then slapped Trell up one more time in a rush to get out of our presence. I seriously felt like Leon was hiding something. I just didn't know what. I mean, if his bitch was ugly or something that was okay. He needed to know we weren't gonna judge him; well… at least I wasn't.

Trell followed me to my room. "Yo, you heard from Abbey?"

I frowned. "Why the fuck you asking me about Abbey? Of course I have… why? You better not be checking for my fucking friend Trell! You know the rules… besides, she won't fuck with you anyway… that's a deal breaker right there, none of us were to fuck with each other's siblings and that's on period."

He waved me off… "Awe man, girl get yo panties out ya ass. I'm just asking cause she was pose to do something for me, but I can't get her on the phone."

I shrugged while pulling my money from my top drawer and adding the money from today inside the envelope. "Well

I don't know about that. I'm supposed to see her this weekend." I informed him. "Right now though, I need you to get out so I can get situated."

"Ain't got to tell me twice..." He chuckled before walking out. "Love you sis."

"Love you too baby..." I let him know.

LEANDRA 'LELE' WELLS

I ended up dozing off after that and was awaken in the middle of the night by Karter calling me. The clock read 2:05am and I just knew she was in labor or something. "Hello?!" I asked in a panic. "Karter? Everything okay girl? Is my godchild alright? What's going on?" I bombarded her with questions while sitting up. Turning the lamp on, I rubbed my eyes.

"Calm down my soul sista…" She giggled. Karter still had the same squeaky voice. "Didn't mean to awaken you boo. Just wanted to check in with you. I'm always up this time of morning anyway and you fell heavy on my mind. How are you?"

I exhaled and rolled my eyes. Like is she serious? How am I? Sleepy as fuck is what I really wanted to say. "I'm okay girl. You almost just gave me a panic attack. Don't be scaring me like that."

"Didn't mean to scare you sista… just wanted you to know…that someday you'll forget the hurt, the reason you cried and what may or may not have caused the pain. You will realize that the secret of being free is not revenge, but letting things unfold in their own way and own time. After all, what matters is not the first, but the last chapter of your life, which shows how well you ran the race. So smile, laugh, forgive, believe, and love all over again for you are a beautiful black Queen and you deserve it."

"Is it scary to say I really needed to hear that?" I wiped a tear that was threatening to fall. "I want to start all over and love again. I really do but I just…"

"Just nothing… your story is still being told." She cut me off. "By the way… I'm having the baby in a few weeks."

I perked up. "Really??? I wish I could come there… I'd have to get permission from my probation officer but I can't promise that. How's the fiancé?"

"He's doing well… doubt anyone would meet him any time soon cause he's always working."

"We wouldn't know because you never talk about him." I mentioned while yawning.

"I'm too busy focusing on raising another black queen."

It was so weird to me how she just goes out of her way to make sure she keeps using the word 'black' like she has a point to prove. Clearly everyone could see what color we were but whatever made Karter happy was okay with me. "Understandable… well get some rest sissy… I love you."

"Love you too Queen… good night." She hung up.

I checked the missed calls on my phone after that and had several from Cass. I must've been sleeping hard as fuck cause I didn't hear any of those calls. I called him back but I didn't get an answer. Since I couldn't sleep after that I hopped up and threw on some long black tights, a colorful sports bra and some bedroom slippers. The house was dark so I tiptoed outside and sat on the porch with my apple air pods in my ear watching the cars ride by since we lived on a main street and the city of Miami never slept anyway.

I mostly sat thinking about my future plans and my goals cause just being a cook wasn't going to cut it for me. I stared at my old car in the driveway that Malik had purchased for me. I'd never get rid of it, but I knew I'd never drive it again. A part of me felt like that car and my engagement ring was all I had left of him. I didn't even have a piece of clothing cause Ms. Jones took it all, she took everything he owned although she didn't pay for any of it. The car she was driving around in right now was one of his. I felt like I'd put in enough time with Malik to be able to have something but I had nothing, while she had the money leftover in the safe which she probably spent by now. On many occasion I wanted to call her but I had to put myself in her shoes. Would I want to talk to the person who was responsible for killing my child? I know I wouldn't. She didn't visit me one time when I was locked up. Didn't send me anything. Didn't respond to any of my letters or nothing…so I knew. I couldn't even blame her. In prison I told myself I'd go see her but being on the streets it was different. I just didn't have the balls.

Deep in my thoughts I was distracted by Cass's truck pulling up in the driveway. He hurriedly turned the lights off and hoped out. He had on a simple pair of grey sweats and a wife beater with some black and white Dolce and Gabbana slides. He smelled like fresh soap and axe when he walked up on me and took a seat on the porch steps like it was 2 in the afternoon. I removed my Air pods from my ears and looked at him like he was crazy. Hell, I wasn't even surprised he didn't have those two big black niggas with him. "Don't tell me you're a damn stalker too."

"I'm not… this the best time of the night though, and it feels good as fuck out here. Look how shit still lit up. People moving around like it's the first part of the day. I love my city man…" He focused on the street and then looked at me. "What you doing out here anyway?"

"I should be asking you that… how did you even know I was out here?"

He shrugged. "I didn't… shit, I was just cruising the streets and couldn't sleep. I just so happened to be coming down yo street and saw you… I tried to call you too."

"Yeah… I was doing what normal people do… sleep." I chuckled. "I just was out here thinking that's all…"

"About what?"

"My future… my plans…"

He nod his head giving me his undivided attention and that deep look he always gave me that gave me chills. Cass always made me feel like he was picking my soul. "What are yo future plans ma? Tell me, I'd like to know…"

Instead of looking back at him. I just stared off into the night sky. "I really don't wanna share right now. I just don't wanna talk about it and just be about it. If you're still around you'll see."

Cass grabbed my hand into his. "Check this out LeLe… I'll be around to see. Nigga don't plan on going nowhere. Ion even know why we keep playing this little game we playing. You scared and I can understand why… but I'm not tryna hurt you."

"It's not even all about that Cass…"

"What is it then?"

I sighed. "Cass, what do I really know about you? I don't even know if you have a girl… do you have a girl or somebody you seeing?"

"Do you see any females around me?"

"No…" I replied.

"Okay then… next question."

"Kids?"

"You ever seen any around me?"

I shook my head 'no'.

"Okay then…" He said. "Let's just stop playing these games and shit. I'm not asking you to go in headfirst with me. I'm just asking you to let me at least put a smile back on your face. You been through a lot ma… you deserve that."

The way my heart fluttered; I couldn't even describe. Nor did I try to pull away from Cass when I felt his lips pressed up against mine. My God, it had been so long since I felt a man's lips pressed up against mine as I allowed his tongue to slip into my mouth. I kissed Cass back without rejecting him. However, when I felt that tingling in between my legs, I had to pull back. Kissing was one thing but fucking was another thing and I knew I just wasn't ready for that. Instead of Cass getting agitated, he pulled me closer to him as we both stared out at the road in our own thoughts.

He broke the silence first. "Whose baby beamer is that?"

"Mine… Malik got it for me but I don't ever want to drive it again. It's too painful. I'm scared to drive period." I admitted.

Cass didn't say anything, he pulled out his ringing phone from his pocket and then ignored the call. The same number called him back another two times before he just placed it on silent. I'm not that dumb to not know that was definitely a woman but I wouldn't dare asked. I stood up and yawned with both my arms above my head. "I'm tired Cass… see you at work tomorrow?"

"I'mma pick you up to take you to breakfast and then we gone make a stop." He stood up pulling his key from his pocket while eyeballing me. He licked his lips. "That ass real fat in them tights. Ion like that shit ma… gone have all these niggas out here tryna see what that's about then imma have to fuck somebody up."

I chuckled. "Whatever Cass.... See you in the morning."

Cass didn't leave until he heard me lock the door behind me. When I fell back asleep. I'm sure I had a smile on my face.

LEANDRA 'LELE' WELLS

Cass picked me up bright and early but it was cool since I was already dressed for work. I had my book of new recipes that I'd created with me too. He was dressed down in yet another suit and I had to laugh to myself cause I always looked like a damn bum up against him when he wore these damn suits. I didn't even understand the purpose of them half of the time. We stopped to the Waffle House first where I ordered me a waffle, pan sausage, eggs, cheese grits, and toast with jelly. Cass ordered a western omelet for himself with a side of hash browns.

When we left there, he took me to a car lot. "What are we doing here?" I asked.

"Get out, I want you to help me pick out a car for my mom." He told me.

"Now Cass, I don't even know your mom, don't know anything about her at all so how am I supposed to know what she likes?" I frowned shielding the sun from my face. I didn't wanna tell him I just really didn't wanna do this right now. My stomach was too damn full to be walking around this big ass lot.

"I mean, you a woman and all women like nice shit so go for it."

We walked around the entire lot and it wasn't one thing that I could say I liked that I hadn't seen too much on the road already… that's until we rolled up on a badass brand-new Audi Q8 fully loaded. "Cass!" I called his name all excited waving him over. "This one right here… it's soooo sexy. I know black is a basic color but omggg look at the stitching in the leather." I pointed out the red stitching on the black leather seats.

He glared inside and looked like he was pleased with what he saw. "Yeah this shit sexy as fuck… this the one right here ma." He kissed me on the cheek and told me to wait for him in the lobby while he handled the paperwork and set everything up for his mother to come pick it up. I couldn't wait for the day I could do something like this for my mother… shit must've felt real good to be able to do this.

After about another 45 minutes Cass came walking out. "Come on." He told me.

When we got outside that same truck was sitting in the parking spot with a huge red bow on it. "Damn that was quick." I laughed. "She must be on the way right now… or you about to have somebody drive it to her with this big ass bow on it."

Cass didn't laugh at all, he just gave me a serious look and tossed me the key. "Nah, she got two cars already. This all on you ma… it's yours."

I swallowed hard feeling both excitement and fear. "Cass stop fucking with me okay? This shit isn't funny nor do I have time for this… now tell me when she's coming to get her truck." I demanded.

He swiped his hand across his beard. "Women man… I swear." He sighed and chuckled. "LeLe it's yours, no bullshit.

If I eat, so do the people who I care about around me. I'm not finna have you walking and keep catching rides and Ubers and shit. Can't trust them muhfuckas."

"Wowwwww!" I shyly smiled. "I mean this a nice gesture but ion want nobody spending this kinda money on me Cass." I think there isn't a woman who would've questioned this gesture but a part of me wanted to build my life back up on my own so I can appreciate it more and wake up every day knowing that no matter what odds I had against me… I did this on my own. "At the same time, I didn't want him to feel as though I was ungrateful."

Cass just blankly stared at me before he handed me the paperwork. "How'd I know that you were gon' be on your independent shit? I know what you're thinking without you even saying it that's why I only dropped half price of what the truck is worth as a deposit. The rest you'll just have to make your payments if that's gone make you feel any better… plus paying on time will help you build credit too so if you do good that'll open more opportunities for you to do other shit aiight ma?"

The way he put it made me smile so big cause I really did want to do shit on my own. I nearly knocked him down on the ground when I hugged him and placed small kisses on his cheek. "Thank you, thank you, thank you!" I giggled and ran back to the truck to open the door. "This is sooooo nice…" I inhaled the new car smell.

"You welcome ma… but you gotta get to Jazzy's now. It's opening time and I got something to do so you gotta drive yourself okay?" He noticed the fear in my eyes when he said that. "You can do this."

I took a deep breath and nod my head before placing my seatbelt on. "You're right, I can do this." I gripped the wheel tightly with both hands. "I can do this." I said again more so just coaching myself.

Cass pulled off and left me here, but there was something I needed to do before I pulled off. I called Abbey. "Bitch get Kim on the line asap and Karter too." I told her.

"Wait hold on bitch calm down…" She chuckled. "I'm just going on break let me walk out of here cause ion want none of these nosey ass patients in my mouth." I heard her walking through the doors until her background noise changed and I heard her getting in her car. She immediately got them on the phone.

"What's up my sistas?" Karter spoke to us. "Heyyy sis…." She then singled out Kim.

"What's good sister? When the baby coming?" Kim asked.

"Soon… real soon. I'm almost nine months so any day now."

"Ohhh okay… so why we all on the phone? We ain't did this shit in a long ass time, which mean somebody got some tea…" said Kim.

"Um hmm it's LeLe, shit she had me call everybody so I'm waiting too, bitch what's up?" Abbey asked all excited rushing me.

"Okay so get this… ya'll know I been kicking it with Cass a lil bit or whatever right… and lately he's been kinda coming at me and I've been ignoring it but he's been laying it on real thick so this morning he comes to pick me up for work and tells me he needs me to go with him to pick out a car for his mother after breakfast."

"Okay…"

"Um hmm…"

"What else Queen?"

Is all I heard while I kept explaining. "I picked out a nice ass Audi Q8 for his mother so he tells me to wait in the lobby while he does the paperwork. I come back out thinking we're about to leave and the same truck has a big ass red bow on it out front. The nigga then tosses me the keys and tells me it's mine!"

"Bitch liesssssss!" Kim squealed. "That nigga got you an Audi truck? Hell nah I know you done gave him some pussy."

"On everything I love I didn't. I haven't done shit like that since I been home. Dust all around my shit." I giggled.

"Girrlllllll.... You in there then... shit that nigga got you a car." Said Abbey.

Karter chimed in. "You deserve everything that puts a smile on your face."

"Omggg I still can't believe this shit ya'll. You know I had to get everybody on the phone at once to tell ya'll this shit."

"Wish a nigga would buy me a car, shit what the fuck am I doing wrong?" Kim sour ass asked.

Abbey sucked her teeth. "This ain't about you Kim, don't you even start your shit."

"Girl, I didn't even do nothing...." She replied to Abbey. "Congrats LeLe, that's what's up."

"Thank you..." I told her. I was so used to Kim replies it didn't even faze me. No matter what she was still my friend.

"You know you gotta send me some pics." Said Abbey.

"Nah better yet you bitches better be dressed tonight I'm coming to pick ya'll up. Ya'll know I don't drink but ya'll can have whatever you like... drinks on me."

"Shittt ain't gotta tell me twice. I'll be ready." Abbey agreed.

"Me too." Kim said.

Karter's pregnant ass couldn't go no damn where even if

she was living here. "Just send me videos ya'll cause ya'll know that my ass misses everything."

"Karter please, nobody told you to haul ass, get cuffed, get pregnant and then hide your life from us like we're some strangers." Kim sassed.

"Whelp sistas… that's my cue to head on out. Congrats again LeLe… I love you all dearly. Have a blessed day." She hung up.

After we indulged in a few more words we all hung up. I had to close my eyes and say a quick prayer before pulling off of the lot but when I did leave I made sure I had on my seatbelt and both hands on the steering wheel. I looked like a teenager taking the damn driving test for the first time as my hands shook when I eased out into traffic. A ride that should've taken me about 15 minutes turned into about 30 minutes. When I made it to Jazzy's I felt like I could breathe again.

I wasn't sure where this thing with Cass and me was going. I just knew in my heart I'd always love Malik and I truly hoped he did forgive me from the other side, but I knew at some point my life did have to go on.

LEON WELLS

"Wells going for the 3 pointer! Can he make it with five seconds on the clock? FIVE, FOUR, THREE, TWO, ONE!"

Swoosh! Nothing but net as the crowd went wild cheering for me. The game was packed and this was the final game before playoffs. It felt good as fuck making the last play of the game putting us up by 6 points. This was one game I invited everybody to and they actually showed up although I waited till the last minute. LeLe was already out with Abbey and Kim about to do their girl shit but they made sure they came to my game first even though they were all dressed up and shit. When I saw Abbey in the stands I couldn't even look her in the eyes nor had I been answering her calls cause I just simply didn't know what to say. I was pissed when I found out Kevin referred to me as his man and shit but knowing Abbey she wouldn't tell shit until she spoke to me… I at least owed her that but tonight wasn't the night.

Trell showed up with Majestic, which kinda fucked with me a lil bit cause it seemed like the more distant I became; the more Majestic tried to pull Trell in. I didn't wanna feel like I was competing for my brother when it came to no nigga at all. I honestly didn't even trust Majestic as much as Trell did anyway.

George wasn't feeling good right before the fourth quarter started so I peeped when him and my mama left early, which was cool. "That was a good ass game brother!" LeLe congratulated me stopping me from walking to the locker room with my team.

"Appreciate that sis." I told her wiping the sweat from my forehead. Abbey and Kim were talking to some other nigga I didn't know.

Trell clapped me up next and then Majestic. "That was a good ass game my boy." Majestic said giving me props.

"Appreciate that..." I told him noticing LeLe and him lock eyes barely speaking to one another... just a nod of the head between the two. Shit was weird as fuck.

When Majestic walked away excusing himself. We followed with our eyes as he walked up on Kim engulfed in a conversation. LeLe spoke up to Trell. "Umm why are you with him so much lately Trell? What's going on?" She questioned him.

Trell wasn't the one to argue. "Why you so pressed man? That nigga ain't did shit to you LeLe."

"It doesn't matter, I know what he does and ion want my little brother wrapped up in that shit. Besides, he hates me. I can see right through that act and ion trust him with you... you can trust him if you want but I'm telling you not to. Keep your eyes open Trell."

"I'm good... and I'll never let nobody fuck with you aiight sis? But I'm my own man now and you gotta let me be just that." He kissed her cheek and walked away.

"Look, I gotta get to the locker room but I appreciate you

for coming." I told her. Once we hugged I walked the opposite direction. Kevin was coming up out of the stands.

"Good game…" he told me acknowledging me waiting for me to respond.

"Thanks, I appreciate that." I told him.

"Heyyyyy Leon…." A group of chicks I recognized from campus came up to me with hugs and congrats on the game. I paid Kevin no mind as I focused on them instead. I know the shit wasn't right but I didn't know what else he wanted me to do. Kevin simply walked away and left us talking. As soon as he did, I dismissed them and went to shower and put on some basketball shorts and a hoodie. When I made it to my car I sat there for a few minutes before heading to the trap.

I made my drop off and counted the dough that was rightfully mine. I knew Kevin was mad at me especially when he didn't answer the phone so I drove to his apartment to see what was up. He opened the door wearing a pair of sweatpants and no shirt. He'd taken his braids out and his hair was out with a crinkly look and a fresh tape. He also had a glass of wine in his hand. He didn't say shit to me, just walked away and left me to lock the door as he went back and sat down on the couch in front of his flat screen that was mounted on the wall. I dropped my duffle bag and sat down next to him. He turned the T.V. down…. "You wanna know something Leon? I've tutored you, cooked for you, never missed a game, dealt with all your rules, the games you play with me… I've even allowed you to treat me like a damn puppet. But today… I'm just tired. Tired of allowing you to make me feel dumb and unwanted and it's simply not fair. Every time we're good you do something to fuck that up. You didn't even want to speak to me today and you asked me to come… you." He pointed to me and then drink the rest of his wine.

I didn't bother to fuss cause he was right. "I been told you that it isn't you… I know it's me so why we doing this again Kevin? I didn't come here for that. Don't you think I know I be fucking up?"

"Can't tell… what's the part that's so hard about this?"

I thought about what Latrell had said the other night about Gays and Queers and shit. "You really wanna know the hardest part of this all? It's the fear of losing my brother Kevin. That's the other half of me. You know how this shit would break him? I don't think the nigga will ever forgive me for this."

"I understand that Leon, but baby… he's gonna go on with his life and be happy with who he wants to be happy with and you're gonna be miserable trying to impress everybody else. We aren't the first gay couple and we won't be the last."

Kevin knew how I felt about him calling me gay so I don't even know why he said that shit but tonight, I didn't wanna argue with him. Instead, I pulled him close to me and allowed him to place his head on my broad shoulder. "It's gone get better Kevin. I promise you that."

"Right… you always say that… so when is it gonna start Leon? Damn I could be out here with plenty dudes who would love to have me but I done gave your thug ass my heart."

"Well…" I looked in his green eyes. "You can start by giving me a kiss." I placed a kiss on his lips before pulling back staring at the ceiling. Being around him felt good. He made me happy even when I didn't wanna be. I didn't wanna lose Kevin or keep doing him like this and I knew it was gonna be a matter of time before he just exploded… or just walked away from me. "I'mma figure it out Kevin… but just know, it's me and you. I'm really not on that shit I'm not playing with no other bitches or none of that."

Kevin was silent but I knew he was thinking to himself. I didn't have to ask him if he loved me cause I knew the answer already. He did. In all honesty I loved him too, just didn't know how to actually come out and say the shit. I had the choice to go home; but tonight like many other nights, I chose to stay with him.

The next morning… he woke up and fixed me breakfast before he went to his study group and when I finished eating, there was something else I needed to do so when I locked up his apartment I hopped in my whip and made my way to North Miami. Abbey wasn't home so I decided to sit on her porch and wait for her. After about 30 minutes she showed up rushing. She had on her work scrubs too. "Boy what the hell are you doing on my porch?" She sassed fumbling with her house keys. "I done got all the way to work and forgot my damn purse." She ran inside and came back out with it.

"Abbey look… I never did get to holla at you about that day when…."

"Leon listen I'm not here to judge you." She said cutting me off. "Now if you're shooting your shit up the dookie chute that's on you and your own personal business but you have to live in your truth. It's not for me to tell it, that's all on you. Now if you wanna finish this conversation I get off at 5:30 and you can come back then!" She hopped in her car and sped off.

I couldn't believe she even said that dumb ass shit to me. Every time I thought about coming out, somebody said some twisted ass shit. Now I understood why niggas just shut the fuck up. Society made it that way. Muhfuckas wanted the truth but look how they acted or shit they said about gays…

shit didn't make no sense. Let me know I'm better with just shutting the fuck up.

Normally I'd get irritated real bad and take it out on Kevin by staying away from him for a couple of days. Today though, I was gonna do something different. Just wanted him to know I appreciated him so I made my way to Aventura Mall to cop him something nice. I just wanted him to know that I really did appreciate him for putting up with my shit. "What up? How's your morning going so far?" I called Kevin when I left the mall.

"Wowww… this is definitely a first." He laughed. "My morning is going just fine baby. Did you enjoy your breakfast?"

"I did… that was nice of you." I tossed the bags on my front seat. "What you doing tonight?"

"Nothing much… home, just like any other time."

"Well, tonight I wanna take you on a date aiight? I'll grab you at about 9pm." I informed him.

I didn't even have to see his face to hear the hopefulness in his voice although he tried to play it cool. "How should I dress?"

"The usual… don't push it Kevin; nigga ain't going all out yet. Just tryna be a man of my word and show you I'm trying. That's all I can do."

"Okay okay… I get it… I'll see you tonight, gotta go."

"Aiight…" I hung up the phone and got back in my whip wondering that the fuck I was gonna do. One thing I did know was that it was time to start looking for my own place so that's what I was gonna get on top of today.

ABBEY DANIELS

I had been calling Leon for days trying to get in contact with him but I guess he wasn't really feeling my comments when he tried to talk to me that day; that and the fact that I was rushing as well. I should have chosen my words better and I wanted to apologize about that had he given me the chance. Fresh off of work I kicked my shoes off and flopped down on the couch before pulling my socks off. I needed a minute to unwind before I poured me a glass of Remy on ice with no chaser. That's the kind of day I had today.

As soon as I was getting ready to do so there was a knock on my door. I started to ignore the shit but I knew that whoever it was would know I was in here since my car was out front. I checked the peephole and spotted Trell standing there. "I know your stubborn ass in there, you just got here too cause the hood on ya car still hot. You probably being petty as fuck staring at me talking shit to you right now."

I covered my mouth from laughing at his silly ass. Served him right. I hadn't answered his calls or given him no pussy since the day he showed up to save me with that bitch in his car. I slowly unlocked the door and stood to the side so he could walk in. “Hurry up and say what you gotta say Trell, cause I got something to do.” I lied.

Trell waved me off, “Girl you ain’t got shit else to do. Why the fuck you ain’t been answering my calls shorty? What the fuck I do now?”

I locked the door crossing both my arms in front of my chest. “You know exactly what the fuck you did.”

He flailed his arms in the air. “Awe man don’t tell me we on this same shit. I explained to you the two options I had that day and I chose you first.” He scratched his head like he was confused. “I thought we went through this on that day. I explained myself to you so what else you want me to say? Damn, nigga can’t get no pussy from you, no conversation, no shit all cause you in yo fucking feelings. You want me to keep everything a secret… cool… I been doing that and letting this shit play out by yo rules. Like damn, my bad for bringing her in yo presence but you already know what it is.”

“First of all you need to calm the fuck down.” I poured me a shot of Remy and swallowed it before giving him the next shot in which he took to the head.

“Nah don’t tell me to calm down… you need to calm down. You women are confusing as fuck. Either you want a relationship with me or you don’t… it’s simple.”

“Oh please… you know that’s not what I want. You know we can’t do that. As a matter of fact don’t even talk to me about relationships Trell cause truth is… niggas say it and do it cause it looks and sounds good. Ya’ll don’t be really ready to put in the blood, sweat and tears that come behind it. Nobody wants to put in that work.”

Trell looked at me licking his lips. “I got some work for you aiight… a whole lot of it too.”

I rolled my eyes trying to play tough and shit but I wanted

to give him some pussy just as bad as he wanted it and I prayed that this was the last time cause this shit had to stop. "I'm done talking anyway. Just keep your hoes at a distance ion wanna see them bitches in my presence."

Trell was so close to me our lips were brushing across each other as he looked down at me. "Just admit that you love me… you feeling some shit bout me you aint pose to feel and I know this cause I'm feeling the shit too. What's the real reason you ain't got a man yet?"

I furrowed my brows at him. "Are you suggesting that I'm waiting for you or something? Cause if so you've got some nerve. I'll never get splinters in my ass waiting on no nigga, especially not you Trell."

He didn't say shit else, instead he just kissed my lips hard as fuck causing my panties to instantly cream up. Just like any other time we fucked right here in the middle of my living room before making our way to the kitchen where he sat me on top of the island spreading my legs wide to feast on my pussy like it was his last super. "Oooooo shitttttt!" I squealed bucking my ass from up under me as he sucked and used the softest, flattest part of his tongue to play with my clitoris until it was hard and swollen. Trell focused on that spot causing me to have one big ass orgasm as my juices slipped off into his mouth.

By the time he finished with me there, I was exhausted but Trell wasn't done. In one swift motion he pulled out his thick pulsating dick before shoving it inside of me with my legs pushed all the way back behind my head. "You gone stop playing with me Abbey!" He groaned looking me dead in the eyes. I tried to turn away as I bit my bottom lip. Trell had me filled up to the max. He was punishing me in the worst way as tears filled my eyes from both pain and pleasure "You know you been wanting some of this daddy dick ma." He leaned down and kissed my lips hard.

"Oh my Godddd Trell…. Ouuuuu… ssssss." I whined and moaned feeling both of his strong hands up under my ass cheeks spreading them apart. I talked big shit to this nigga all the time and yet I couldn't even handle his young ass. Had me folded up like a pretzel with tears and shit in my eyes. "Nigga this shit feel soooo…oh my… and why you aint put on a condom?" I felt my eyes roll to the back of my head cause he started hitting it harder until the hook on his dick found my G-Spot.

I couldn't hold it anymore… I was creaming all over his dick long and hard when I felt him shooting up in me. "Ahhhh fuck ma!" He held me still until he let his all-out collapsing on top of me. I didn't move nor try to stop him. I just lay here enjoying his scent and everything about him. Trell's ass had me gone and I tried so damn hard to ignore it.

When he finally got up he went to the bathroom and got a wet cloth and took his time wiping me up before he helped me up and down off the island. I cleaned him up next. "What you bout to do?" He asked me.

I took my time putting my clothes on. "I don't know but I know what you're about to do… go get me a damn plan B."

Trell chuckled. "I knew that was coming… I'll get it. Just ride with me somewhere first… please?" He asked giving me a sad ass puppy dog face right when I was all prepared to say no.

I sighed. "Aiight I'll ride with you but have me back in the next few hours Trell cause I'm tired as hell and I have to be to work super early tomorrow."

"I got you…" He told me.

I rode with Trell until we pulled up to a barber shop in Carol City. "I know you didn't have me come ride with you just so you can get a fresh tape? Nigga I could've stayed home."

He looked in the mirror and examined his dreads. "Nah, I'm bout to cut it all off. It gotta go Abbey. Nigga bout to graduate soon and I don't want these folks fucking with me cause I'm one of the faces of the race… same shit they look for… young, black, dreads, tattoos… nah… I'm good. These muhfuckin' cops getting outta control. Every time I watch the news its some fuck shit… and make it so bad ain't no justice…. But when a nigga hold court in the streets we get locked the fuck up like some animals."

"Sometime our people are so stupid… it ain't always folks just picking cause as a race we gotta do better." I told him. "But I definitely agree with you and understand what you're saying." I explained as we got out of the car. We walked into the barber shop and Trell sat down in the chair. I still can't believe his ass did it. He was fine as hell before but he was beyond handsome now and it was scary how much Leon and him looked alike. The only thing that separated them before was the dreads but now that Trell cut his off and now rocked a low boy like Leon… they could easily be mixed up to the naked eyes.

"What you gone do with that bag of hair?" I pointed to all the dreadlocks they'd cut off.

"Shit I'mma keep it for memories. Nigga nearly cried like a bitch in that chair when he started cutting but it's for the best. I had to be a G bout this shit and remember what I was doing it for." He tossed me the keys. "Here… you drive, I need to make some phone calls."

I did as he ask while laughing at him at the same time. Dawning on me at the last minute I decided that I wanted to do something nice for him like cook him dinner or something. I kinda felt weak as fuck cause I ain't never in my life cooked for no nigga before but since Trell played by all of my rules most of the time… it was the least I could do. "I'mma cook for you tonight if you ain't busy; and I'm warning you don't get used to this shit… I'm just being nice."

Trell gave me a knowing smirk. "You can cook whatever you want for me as long as it ain't no spaghetti. I don't trust ya'll women around that red sauce. Got me fucked up."

I bust out laughing. "Boy! I'm not even on my period… what the fuck? I'd never do that nasty ass shit anyway."

"Yeah… aiight." He said in all seriousness.

"Imma make you some lemon butter salmon, yellow rice and veggies but I gotta stop at Publix first to get everything I need. You coming in with me?" I asked.

He shrugged… "Yeah… I mean, I'm not the one hiding."

I ignored his comment and walked in the store. I wanted to pay for everything but he refused to let me and paid instead. On the way out we were almost to the car when we heard somebody behind us talking shit. "You lying motherfucker!" We turned around just in time to see the light skin green eyed nigga swinging on Trell. I remembered his face. It was Kevin.

He was quick on his feet ducking the blow. "Yo what the fuck? Nigga you done lost yo muthafuckin mind? You tryna get killed?" Trell went from sweet to killer instinct. I was in shock watching this shit play out in front of me like a movie.

"You're a lying piece of shit! All that shit you talk! All that shit about you trying to prove yourself… then what the fuck are you doing hugged up with her in the store?" He asked referring to me. It took a minute for me to even register what the hell was going on. *Oh my god!* I thought to myself… he must think Trell is Leon with this haircut. I wanted to intervene but before I could Kevin was swinging again catching Trell on the side of his face.

"Oh Hell naw! Fuck his ass up Trell!" I snapped when Trell grabbed Kevin by the neck using the other hand catching him in the jaw. Trell beat Kevin ass so badly he was on the ground in a fetal position trying to block the blows while people stood around recording and shit on their phones. "Trell that's enough you gone kill him!" I tried pulling him off of him watching Kevin's light skin turn purple and black. Blood was on the concrete too from his nose and mouth. "Trell!" I slapped his face to get him out of his daze, must've been a little too hard cause he looked up like a wild animal grabbing me by the neck.

"The fuck you slap me for?" He growled.

I removed his hand from around my neck. "Get your fucking hands off of me Trell! You wanna go to jail for murder? Cause you gone kill his ass!"

Poor Kevin didn't even wanna move as he slowly looked up with swollen eyes and a busted lip… his jaw was swollen on one side. "Tr…Tr…Trell?" He asked confused. "You're Trell?"

Trell looked at him with death in his eyes. "The fuck I'm pose to be nigga?!" He was ready to fuck his ass up again.

"Forget it, let's just go aiight?" I pulled on Trell grabbing the bags. This isn't the way I wanted him to find out about his brother… not like this. I heard the sirens in a distance. "Trell we gotta go!" I pulled until he finally followed me. He didn't say shit to me, just hopped in the passenger side without another word. When we rode past Kevin, people were helping him up as him and me locked eyes. Trell had truly fucked him up. I prayed that Trell didn't think too much into it and just took it as mistaken identity cause if not this wasn't about to be good.

The entire time I cooked, Trell sat at the table watching me still trying to get control of his attitude cause he was still pissed. I know I looked cool on the outside but on the inside I was screaming 'what the fuckkkkk!' cause that shit was wild and crazy and I just couldn't believe I witnessed that shit. I wanted to call LeLe so bad and tell her what was up but I couldn't do it. Mainly because LeLe didn't know shit but as soon as Trell left I was calling Leon to tell him what happened and I prayed he answered. "You okay?" I asked Trell.

"I told you about putting yo hands on me Abbey…"

"Well what did you want me to do? Let you go to jail? Cause I wasn't about to do that. Yes, I slapped you. I'll slap your ass again if it's gone keep you out of jail. You better hope and pray that nobody gave them crackers your fucking tag number."

He looked like he was in deep thought…. "I wonder who the fuck that fuck ass nigga thought I was…" He stared off into his own thoughts… then he looked back at me. "You don't think he could've thought…." He paused and stopped himself. "Nah…. Fuck nah…"

"What?" I asked.

"Nothing… just had a dumb ass thought that's all." He dismissed whatever he was thinking. I had a feeling though. My insides were screaming, cussing, and fucking hollering. "The food almost ready? I'm hungry…"

I nod my head. "Yeah… in a few minutes." I walked away from the stove and poured him a glass of Remy on ice and chased it with a little red bull I had left over in the fridge. "Drink this in the meantime and calm your nerves."

He took the glass and took it to the head. When the food was done I fixed his plate and sat it in front of him. "I'm going to shower, I'll be back." I slipped off and went to shower. Before I got in I called Kim but she didn't answer and I know her miserable ass was probably sitting there staring at the fucking phone.

Fuck it… I mumbled and hopped in letting the water cascade down my body just taking it all in. After I hopped out I snuck and called Leon to let him know what happened and to tell him he better check on his boy but he didn't answer. I was probably wrong for telling Trell to fuck Kevin up although he was gonna do that anyway the minute Kevin put his hands on him, but I'm a firm believer that if a muthafucka put hands on you… you better had touched they ass back and properly too. When I headed back into the kitchen Trell was finished eating and washing out his plate. There was nothing left on it so I assume it was good and I was proud of myself. "Like it?"

"Yeah ma… that shit was fie…" He answered just like the Miami nigga that he was. He picked up his cell phone and answered an incoming call. "Ma… what's up? I hope you ain't calling me for no money to take to bingo cause I'm not contributing to that no more. You don't never win; you need to give it up." He told her listening intensely to what she was saying. His face went from perplexed to worried. "Wait… George what? What hospital? I'm on my way." He hung up.

Now I was worried. "What happened?"

He looked at me with so much fear in his eyes. "George had a heart attack… I gotta get to the hospital… you coming?"

I nibbled on my bottom lip knowing that LeLe had gotten the same call, and she would probably be there and the last thing I wanted to do was show up with Trell. "No… you go. I'll drive myself." I told him.

Trell just looked at me and shook his head before heading out without another word. I grabbed my keys and my coat answering my own cell phone. It was LeLe. "Hey boo…" I answered trying to play cool knowing what she was calling me to tell me already.

I could tell she was crying. "I need you to meet me at the hospital… George had a heart attack."

"Say less babes and it's gone be alright. I'm on my way. Which hospital?"

"Aventura…"

"Okay, I'll meet you there." I hung up feeling bad as fuck. None the less, I rushed out to be there for my friend.

KIMBERLY 'KIM' LAWS

I didn't know why the fuck everyone was blowing up my phone cause I had my own shit I was dealing with. For the past few hours I had gotten high as a kite. Shit was bad. I had my good days and I had my bad days. Today was just one of those days. As bad as I despised Karter, I just really wanted to talk to her on a sisterly level. However, I tried calling my mama first. "Hey what's up Kim?" My mama answered the phone.

"Hey…" I spoke dryly. "Just wanted to say hi and see what's up with you. How you been? Figured I'd ask since nobody checks on me."

"Oh Kim please… don't you even start that cause your fingers work just as good as anyone else's. Hell, I'm the mama… I raised you. You should be calling me not me chasing you."

I rolled my eyes. "I'm just saying… I guarantee Karter gets a call at least a few times a week."

"Are we really going to start this again? Karter is about to have my grandchild any day now so I'm sorry if you feel a certain kind of way but of course I'm going to call her to check on them." She informed.

I didn't even want to argue with her so I left that well enough alone. "Whatever… what you doing anyway?"

She sighed. "Actually I'm headed on over to meet Brian at the doctor. I didn't tell you cause we haven't spoken but he slipped and fell on the job and broke his hip. Ended up having to have a total hip replacement." She spoke of my stepfather.

I burst into a long ass laughter.

"Kim! I know damn well you aren't sitting on this phone laughing! What the fuck is so funny about that?!"

"Nothing besides he should've broke both his fucking hips… maybe he will finally learn to keep his nasty ass hands off of peoples young daughters." I was still laughing. Mostly trying to disguise the pain.

"KIMBERLY! I CAN'T BELIEVE YOU'RE STILL HOLDING ON TO THIS STORY! YOU'VE BEEN LYING ALL YOUR DAMN LIFE AND YOU'RE STILL GOING! YOU'VE BEEN DYING FOR ATTENTION SINCE FOREVER AND I WISH YOU JUST FOUND A MAN TO GIVE IT TO YOU CAUSE MY MAN IS MINE AND I'M NOT GONE LET YOU TARNISH HIS NAME. ESPECIALLY WHEN HE HELPED ME RAISE AND PROVIDE FOR YOUR UNGRATEFUL ASS."

"It's just so unfortunate that you think that ma… but whatever, your husband… your problem. You don't ever have to believe me. I'm grown now so it is what it is. Just know it's mothers like you that make it hard for girls like me to speak their truth cause you put a nigga before your child."

"You have some serious issues girl… and I truly pray that one day you get the help that you need. Good night Kim." She hung up in my face.

I continued to laugh and wiped a tear from my eye. I was so over this shit. I had so much I needed to get off of my chest. So many things I wanted to confess. I know I need help. Shit it wasn't no damn secret. I found my favorite white bag of powder and rubbed a little inside my mouth on my cheeks for the third time today and then I called Karter. She didn't pick up so I left a message for her. "Hey girl… I know you're probably busy doing the mommy and wife shit but I really need to drive up there. I need to talk to you. I'm coming tonight okay? Make sure you call me back." I hung up and started to pack me a little bag.

I stared at my ringing cell phone five minutes later thinking it was Karter but it wasn't. Instead it was LeLe; I ignored it. Next it was Abbey; I ignored her too. They were probably just calling to have a girl's night or some shit but I wasn't in the mood. I didn't want to hear about their perfect lives and how well shit was going. I just wasn't beat for that shit tonight. I rushed to take me a shower and then grabbed me a cold wine cooler from the fridge after I got dressed. I then went out on my balcony and smoked me a fat ass joint. Majestic had been blowing my phone up but it had been so hard trying to ignore what I was feeling for him lately without feeling sorry for the shit I'd done since I was a part of his pain.

Grabbing my bag, I turned off all of the lights and turned my alarm on before getting in my car and hitting the highway. If I didn't get this shit off of my chest I was going to explode. Karter would just have to be mad with me for showing up unannounced but oh fucking well…. She should've called me back. I made sure to stop at the local Speedway and gas up first. Once I did that; I sat in the car for another ten minutes at the pump just thinking. My tints were black as hell… illegally black too so I knew nobody could see me anyway. Today was such a horrible day. When those demons started talking to me; I just couldn't get it to stop. *Come on Karter call me back...* I mumbled to myself.

It seemed like a never-ending wait, so I took a deep breath and prepared to take my 3 ½ hour ride all by my lonesome. Just me, my thoughts, and my bullshit. An hour into my ride and I was already tired and regretting that I didn't just take the Mega Bus to Orlando instead of trying to drive. I pulled into a rest area in hopes of taking a nap but my phone just wouldn't stop. "What Abbey? Damn somebody better be dead the way ya'll keep calling me."

"First of all if somebody were dead you'd clearly be the last bitch to know. Why the fuck is it so hard to pick up your phone?"

"I'm trying to get to Orlando to surprise Karter." I told half the truth. "Why?"

"George had a heart attack... can you please please please come up here? You know that man has been good to us all and played the father figure whenever we needed him to. How far are you?" She asked.

"Are you serious?" My heart dropped. Despite anything else. I had a lot of love for George cause he was a good man in general. "I'm barely an hour out. I'mma turn around."

"Omg thank you Kim... hurry up. I appreciate you so much for this. It's not looking good and I'm still waiting for LeLe to get here. I promise we can drive up together in a few days to surprise Karter. I'll go with you. I'll even drive."

"No worries Abbey... I'm coming. It'll be about an hour or so." I assured her.

"Okay drive safe... I love you."

"Love you too." I told her before disconnecting the call and hopping on the highway to head back South. It wasn't often I found myself ready to let it all out but tonight God had other plans so I'd just have to see Karter another day. I turned the music all the way up and drove to Aventura hospital to be a part of George's support system.

By the time I arrived everyone was already waiting in the lobby area and Mrs. Latia was crying her eyes out. I scanned the room and still didn't see LeLe so I made my way to Abbey and Mrs. Latia to get some answers. Deep inside though, I prayed that George was okay. I didn't want LeLe to have to feel that kind of pain cause I know she really appreciated George for taking care of her and never turning his back on her. I knew this was about to be one long ass night.

LEANDRA 'LELE' WELLS

When I got the news of George having a heart attack I immediately went into panic mode. I'd been cuddled up on the couch with Cass watching Black Panther, while eating some popcorn and drinking some wine. He drank a Heineken and munch on some cookies-n-cream Hershey bars since that was his thing. We'd been spending a lot of time together lately but what impressed me the most was that he never pressured with sex or tried to make me feel like I owed him something. Day by day I was feeling that open wound in my heart closing.

I knew when I picked up the phone and heard my mama crying something was wrong. For whatever reason, I knew she was gonna say George before she even called his name and my heart sank to my ass thinking she was about to tell me he was dead. Lord, knows I wasn't prepared for that. That man had been here for me in every way possible so to lose him would be like losing another part of me. "I'm on my way ma! I'll be there soon." I panicked hopping up searching for the shoes I'd worn.

"What's up LeLe… what happen?" Cass asked me looking concerned.

"My father just had a heart attack and I need to get to Aventura hospital…" I told him with my voice cracking. I was so scared for him.

Cass didn't ask me anything else, he simply grabbed my keys off of the counter and then slid on his Gucci slides and his jacket since he already had his jeans on. "I'll drive you."

"You don't have to do that… this is a family issue."

"The fuck does that mean? You don't need to be driving alone in the condition you in all worried and shit so I'll take you. If you want me to bounce after I will… I'll come back and get you when you call."

I thought about what he said… it only took me a second to agree. "Those two big ass black niggas ain't going Cass." I referred to his bodyguards who were outside who never seemed to go too far. I still didn't understand why he even needed them. I liked Cass… a whole lot but I felt there was some shit with him that he was hiding and if he wasn't being truthful with me than we were gonna have a real big problem.

"Cool… they don't have to go… let's ride." He told me.

We walked out of the house together and were met with a set of headlights pulling up. A young, tall, dark skinned Barbie looking girl hopped out of royal blue and white Wraith dressed in designer and iced out. "Who is that?" I asked.

"What's good CoCo?" Cass asked her.

She looked him up and down. "Oh… you Cass today huh?" She smirked and rolled her eyes ignoring me. "Look man, the hot water heater is out and the garbage disposal fucking up."

"So… did you call Patrick? You know he handles all the maintenance for me."

"Now if he was answering, do you think I'd driveway over here?" She answered him like that was a no brainer and then she finally acknowledged me holding out her hand to shake mine. "Hey… my name is CoCo… I'm Trey's sister."

"Oh Okay…" I smiled kinda relieved inside. "I'm LeLe… nice to meet you."

She nod her head and focused back on Cass… "Call him, or send somebody else. Please and thank you." She rolled her eyes like she really couldn't stand him and got back in her Wraith speeding off playing her music real loud.

Cass just stared at the lights until he couldn't see the car anymore. I could tell he wasn't pleased about her popping up. "Sorry about that… come on."

We both hopped in the truck and pulled off heading to the hospital. "You own other properties?" I asked since he never mentioned it. He only told me about the one other big ass house he had.

He didn't respond verbally. He only nod his head and drove us to where we needed to go. He held my hand the entire way until we made it to the hospital. He pulled to the front entrance to let me out. "You sure you gon' be okay?" He asked.

"Yeah… go ahead. I'll call you. I just need to make sure my family is good." I assured him and after making sure that I was okay… he pulled off. I hoped he understood that I wasn't just being a bitch by not letting him stay. I just didn't want everyone in my business. This whole situation with Cass and me was just different and deep down inside. I was still dealing with my heartbreak. Although it did get better day by day; it still was a pain that never went anywhere.

I gave the security my I.D to scan to create me a badge and after the information desk told me what floor he was on; I took the elevator up there. My mama, Abbey, Kim, and Trell were all sitting in the waiting area. I ran to my mom wrapping my arms around her. "How is he mama?"

Still visibly shaken up, I could tell she was trying to be strong. "I.. I.. don't know LeLe… he told me he wasn't feeling well and I should've listened. I wouldn't leave bingo when he asked me to and by the time I got home, I hadn't even made it through the front door good and he fell out on the floor grabbing the left side of his chest. The pain on his face told me something was wrong and his pulse was weak so I called the ambulance. It wasn't until we got here that they told me he'd suffered a heart attack from some kind of blockage. He's in surgery now." She wiped her tears. "I was supposed to be there for my husband but I chose to sit in front of a damn Bingo table."

I wasn't even gonna sit here and throw rocks or pour salt on an open wound cause truth is, what she's saying is right. She should've been there. "Thank ya'll for coming." I smiled at Abbey and Kim. Nothing about our friendship was perfect but we always seemed to come together when it mattered the most. Kim was bat shit crazy to me but deep down inside she had a good heart. She just acted out cause she didn't know any better.

Abbey took a swig from her soda. "You know we had to be here girl… don't be thanking us."

"Right…" Kim agreed sitting with her legs crossed in the chair. Lately her ass always looked high. I can guarantee she probably smoked a joint on the way here.

Trell sat off in a chair all by himself scrolling through his phone. I stood up and grabbed his hand to pull him up. "Walk with me…"

He stood up. "What's good sis?"

"Umm has anybody called Leon? Why isn't he here? I was expecting him to be here. I know he has his own life going on but this shit isn't acceptable at all and I'm gonna tell him how I feel."

"Man I been calling that nigga for the last hour. Shit, he won't even pick up for me. He probably on the court somewhere hooping or making a money move. That's the only way I can see him not answering."

"Money move?" I frowned.

He sighed. "Just mind ya business sis… you gotta let a man be a man."

"Trell, I really hope ya'll aint out here doing no illegal shit cause ion want that shit around me and I'm really watching the company I keep. I don't care if ya'll are my brothers."

"Damn… whatever happened to being yo brother's keeper?" He shrugged.

"That's always Trell… you know what I meant so don't play with me. All I'm saying is don't do shit around me… help me stay out of jail. I can't afford to be violated cause I'm cased up off somebody else shit."

He nod his head in agreement. "I got you sis."

We found ourselves in the elevator heading back down to the first floor to go outside and get some fresh air. As soon as we stepped off the elevator Leon was coming from the opposite direction and had already had a visitor tag stuck to his shirt. "Oh look… there goes Leon." I pointed.

We were both relieved to see him but he wasn't smiling at neither one of us. As a matter of fact he was focused on Trell with a mean mug. I'd never seen him looking the way he was looking right now. As he got closer the elevator next to us dinged and Abbey and Kim came off of that one. "What ya'll doing down here? Your mama told us to come get ya'll cause George just came out of surgery..." She paused noticing Leon... "what the fuck is wrong with him?" Abbey frowned and then it was like a light switch went off in her head as he got closer. "Oh shit... oh shit..." she tried to grab Leon. "Leon noooo!"

Too late, she didn't move quick enough before the left side of Trell's face was being met with Leon's right fist. That one hit caused a big ass fight. Trell didn't even know why they were fighting in the first place. We tried so hard to break the shit up as the nurses called for security but it was only so much our little asses could do compared to the size of them. "Stop ya'll!" I yelled. "What the fuck is going on here!"

Abbey tried too hard to get ahold of the situation that she was sweating. Security and the cops were running from both directions grabbing both my brothers in a choke hold as they spoke to each other through their eyes. They looked like they wanted to kill each other as they were being hauled off in cuffs. "Omgggg like whyyy man." Abbey shook her head placing her face in the palm of her hands.

I was out of breath. "Why what? Abbey what the fuck is going on?" My chest heaved up and down.

"Trell beat up Leon's boyfriend but Trell didn't actually know that was Leon's boyfriend." She sighed.

"Boyfriend?" I asked confused knowing damn well she had lost her mind. "Leon don't have no damn boyfriend. My brother ain't gay."

She nod her head. "He is LeLe... he's gay."

"HA!" Kim laughed like it was funny. "Where's the popcorn? This is better than Maury!"

"SHUT THE FUCK UP KIM!" We both yelled at her in unison just as my mama was getting off the elevator wondering where everyone was.

One look at us and she knew something was very wrong. “LeLe… what’s going on?”

As if she needed anymore problems right now… I had to figure out how to tell her Leon is gay and both her boys just got locked up. What a fucking day!

To Be Continued……

GRAB THE NEXT PART

This is a four part series. Be sure to read the rest.

THANK YOU FOR READING

Printed in the USA
CPSIA information can be obtained
at www.ICGtesting.com
CBHW050227081223
2484CB00006B/162